PRAISE FOR J

"Unlike zombies, this book never ambles or staggers!"

—*The Frightened Whisper*

"Brilliant! Fun and thought-provoking! Like a pajama party pillow fight!"

—Hot Young Girls

"The definitive document on the age-old ninja/pirate rivalry."

—*Argh*

"If this book doesn't make you laugh, you must be undead! Seriously. Separate yourself from your loved ones because you almost certainly pose a danger to them."

—*Epidemiology This Week*

"The ideas contained within this novel pose a threat to our way of non-life."

—We, The Zombies

JAMES MARSHALL

NINJA VERSUS PIRATE FEATURING ZOMBIES

ChiZine Publications

FIRST EDITION

Library and Archives Canada Cataloguing in Publication

Marshall, James, 1973-
     Ninja versus pirate featuring zombies / James Marshall.

(The how to end human suffering series ; 1)
Issued also in electronic formats.
ISBN 978-1-926851-58-7

     I. Title. II. Series: Marshall, James, 1973- . How to end
human suffering series ; 1.

PS8626.A78N56 2012   C813'.6   C2012-900419-7

CHIZINE PUBLICATIONS
Toronto, Canada
www.chizinepub.com
info@chizinepub.com

Edited and copyedited by Brett Savory
Proofread by Samantha Beiko

Canada Council   Conseil des Arts
for the Arts   du Canada

BRITISH COLUMBIA
ARTS COUNCIL
An agency of the Province of British Columbia

We acknowledge the support of the Canada Council for the Arts which last year
invested $20.1 million in writing and publishing throughout Canada.

ONTARIO ARTS COUNCIL
CONSEIL DES ARTS DE L'ONTARIO

NINJA VERSUS PIRATE FEATURING ZOMBIES

PROLOGUE:
What's Past is Not;
Nor Will It Ever Be

One day I recognized I was a prisoner in my parents' basement, which I thought was the real world, but it wasn't the real world; it was my parents' basement, and once I realized I was a prisoner in my parents' basement, okay, I didn't realize it was my parents' basement right away, and to be perfectly honest, I wasn't fully aware I was even being held prisoner and, in the interests of full disclosure, I'm not entirely sure how I ever realize anything at any given time, I just do, or seem to, and anyway, I basically woke up, not that I was asleep exactly, but it definitely wasn't a state of full consciousness, and I'm not arguing I'm fully conscious now; I'm merely suggesting I'm more conscious than I was then, and anyway, when I woke up (the whole sleep/waking thing is a metaphor), I noticed I was bound, like, with chains, so I hung out for a while, waiting to see if anything sexy was going to happen, and then, all of sudden, out of nowhere, and to my complete amazement, it totally didn't, so I decided my situation was lame, and I looked around and saw the entire human population of the planet Earth was stuck there in my parents' basement with me (I still didn't know it was my parents' basement), and they, the entire population of planet Earth, were all frantically but soundlessly bashing keyboards that weren't attached to anything, shaking wireless mice beaming invisible signals nowhere, and yelling, but wordlessly, into headsets that weren't connected to anything, bound and determined to remain completely chained-up, staring straight ahead at a huge screen where a bunch of shapes, figures, and forms were displayed, and these shapes, figures, and forms were what—I realized this later—they were what I'd always believed to be real, and they were what the whole world continued to believe was real, and I looked at the whole world chained up in my parents' damp, dank, dark basement and, even though everyone's eyes were wide open, they were, to bring back the metaphor, sleeping, or, at the very least, not fully conscious and, if it isn't already obvious, when you're trapped in my parents' basement, it's like you're dreaming, but you're absolutely convinced you're awake and everything you're experiencing is real—it's all there is, was, and ever could be—but you don't notice the chains binding you, or that you're trapped in your parents' stupid, stinking basement (I'm bitter about the basement now), and as soon as I realized I was being restrained and nothing sexy was going on, I struggled to free myself so I could find some suckers to punish and fools to beat-down for holding me hostage, and when I got loose, I tried to rescue/ wake up some of the people who were trapped nearby, and okay, maybe I focused primarily on the hot young girls initially but it doesn't matter because nobody woke up, and it was then—okay it was a little while later; first I thought about just saving myself—but it was right after that that I knew I had to do something big, dramatic, and important to save the world, and I knew it was going to make me really popular, get me laid lots, and make me very, very wealthy, so feeling pretty good about myself, I left the basement (it had a rapid transit system), even though I still didn't know it was the basement and, en route, with the wind rushing through my heroic hair and over my brave face (it was sort of an open-roof rapid transit system), I passed into another room in the basement, the utility room, where I saw the figures, shapes, and forms again—the ones that were displayed on the big screen that the whole world was staring at, believing they were impacting with their keyboards, mice, and headsets, in the other room—but here, I saw the figures, shapes, and forms in a different way, a three-dimensional way, but they were all covered in tight black cloth and there were little white dots stuck to them all over in what appeared to be strategic locations, and the rapid transit system slowed because I wanted to stop here (it was thought-powered apparently), since at that moment I believed I'd entered the *real* real world, where everything was authentic, true, and legitimate, and it was so beautiful, a valiant tear bulged muscularly over my lower eyelid and rolled triumphantly down my fearless face, but then I noticed everything was being filmed by zombies who were broadcasting it, presumably to the other room in the basement where the whole world was watching it on the LCD display, and the zombies noticed me, Guy Boy Man, gallantly looking at them, and they started ambling in my direction, so I got the hell out of there, but in cool way, and the high-speed convertible train raced me toward a pinprick of piercing white light at the top of a gigantic staircase, and the light grew more and more blinding as I ascended the stairs and passed through the open doorway, leaving behind the basement (that's when I realized it'd been a basement), and I sped through the kitchen, and then the front room where my parents were watching TV (that's when I realized it'd been my *parents'* basement), and then the foyer, racing toward the front door, and the light, which was already painfully bright, grew brighter and brighter until I closed my eyes and covered them with my forearm and suddenly I was transported outside the house, leaving the entire population of the planet behind me, and when my eyes adjusted, I gawked, open-mouthed in awe at the real world, and I saw everything, the animals and the trees, for example, as they are, alive and endangered, obviously, because of climate change, but I saw the animals and trees for what they truly are, dying, gasping-for-breath *beings*, instead of two-dimensional images of shapes, figures, and forms on an LCD display, or three-dimensional representations of the real deal being motion-captured by zombies, and I resolved, resolutely, to return to this abomination, this degradation, this house with its stupid, stinking basement, to free everyone, starting with the hot young girls, and I set off, stout-hearted and determined (by my genetics, upbringing, experiences, and the strange age into which I was born) to save the world.

*"I'm your saviour;
I've come here to destroy you."*

Guy Boy Man

CHAPTER ONE:

Aside From Her Big Breasts, Pale Blue Lips, Child-Bearing Hips, Baby-Powder-White Skin, Cotton-Candy-Pink-Hair, And The Unicorn That Follows Her Everywhere, Baby Doll15 Seems Like Just A Regular Fifteen-year-Old Girl

I'm American so I believe in God. I mean, even if people "invented" God instead of the other way around, God is "real" as far as I'm concerned. Just because something didn't exist *before* you invented it doesn't mean it doesn't exist *after* you invented it. You don't stand in front of a speeding car because it's an "invention" and there was a time when it didn't exist. No. You get the hell out of the way.

It's first thing in the morning and I'm at Scare City High School and the hallway is full of living human teenagers and zombie teenagers so I pull out a half-empty bottle of whiskey, undo the top, take a swig, and lean back against the lockers.

The hallway is a horror show. It's dark. Fluorescent lights flicker off and on, illuminating the nightmare sporadically. Broken bits of (not really) ceiling cover the floor. Failed water pipes spill out. What isn't covered with hazardous rubble is treacherously slippery. Over our heads, insulation is exposed and dangling, like we are, in the heights of uncertainty, over the long deadly fall of discovery, in the futile hope of being helped, and the rectangular metal boxes, which house the bare fluorescent bulbs, hang unevenly from taut wires crimped around sharp metal corners. The destiny of the wires is knowable.

As is ours.

Allow me to introduce myself. I'm Guy Boy Man, which, I admit, is pretty weird, because I'm not Asian, or a series of keywords to search for gay porn, or heterosexual porn, I guess, if you're a chick and you're into porn and if you are, let me just say, that's awesome. I'm sixteen years old and I'm in the tenth grade, which is super convenient if you're into underage girls like I am. Recently I became fantastically wealthy. So that's nice.

In the interests of full-disclosure, I may have, inadvertently, caused a crisis in the global financial system in the process of becoming fantastically wealthy. When I, through a series of exciting adventures I can't be bothered to relate here, gained access to unspeakable wealth—I actually like to talk about it but it turns out a lot of people don't want to hear about it—I, unfortunately, [or fortunately if you're me (and I am)] caused, it seems, trillions (and trillions) of dollars to be transferred from various (zombie) financial institutions—in fairness, they were being horribly mismanaged and their CEOs were receiving obnoxious salaries—to my personal account, and I did all this while standing in front of an ATM machine—as you can imagine, the people waiting behind me were a little annoyed—but everything is possible, and more than that, necessary.

My fateful trip to the ATM created staggering zombie

unemployment and mind-blowing deficits for zombie governments everywhere. Now hordes of mindless undead monsters Occupy Wall Street and protest in cities around the world. (FYI: I'm 99% of the 1%.)

Where did all these zombies come from? Invariably, zombie outbreaks occur when you're in the hospital. And I *was* in a coma of sorts: I didn't think people were that bad. Oh sure, I knew there was greed and war and religious-mass-media deception. And, of course, I was aware of the poverty, pollution, and corruption. But I thought that was just the way things were. I didn't think there was anything anyone could do about it.

Recently, however, something happened which exposed the fundamentally irredeemable nature of people to me. It made such an impression, I decided to take matters into my own hands and wipe people off the face of the planet Dearth. One of my teachers visited my parents' house one evening. I managed to eavesdrop on Mrs. Miriam Burnett informing my mom and dad that I was destined to perform exceedingly poorly on an upcoming standardized test. Now there's something you should know about me. Until this point, I'd suffered from a problem. Okay, I'd suffered from more than one problem but I'm talking about this one problem in particular. It was called Pre-Traumatic Stress Disorder. I suffered from constant anxiety and depression resulting from the knowledge that, one day, I was going to experience a highly traumatic event. I didn't know what this event was going to be or when it would occur. All I knew was that it was going to be really, really bad.

The traumatic event I'd been waiting for was when Mrs. Burnett told my parents I was going to blow this standardized test. I underwent a profound change. I realized this standardized test wasn't just any standardized test. It was the ZAT: the Zombie Acceptance Test. (Those who pass become zombies and those who don't become zombie food.) I realized my parents weren't my parents and Mrs. Burnett wasn't Mrs. Burnett. They were zombies. Pretty much everyone who was "good" and "moral" and "responsible" is a zombie.

With horror, I listened as my parents and Mrs. Burnett agreed they might as well just eat me right then and there.

Suddenly I realized people/zombies are a scourge!

I confronted my parents and Mrs. Burnett. They were sitting in the (not really) living room. Their slack jaws hung. Their blank white eyes stared. I saw their broken teeth. Sharp and vicious. I saw their blue tongues. Thick drool slow-oozed from the sides of their mouths: viscous. Their skin was the colour grey would be if grey turned grey. It was cracked in places and old-wound purple. I didn't say anything to them.

I didn't have anything to say.

In one hand, I had a hatchet. In the other hand, I had a video camera.

Walking toward them, I lifted the hatchet.

While decapitating my zombie parents, in the process of progress, I separated their mealy-mouths from their sour stomachs. Regardless of the surprise-attacking, the hardcore hacking—working the hatchet forwards and backwards so it would come loose, bracing myself against their stiff bodies with one hand and one foot for leverage and then, wide-eyed, swinging, again and again, my weapon of no-choice through the air, chopping into their necks, bathing me in their toxic blood—my parents groaned in an unfeeling way.

"Back in my day, we didn't have time to decapitate our parents," said my dad. "We had to get to *work*."

JAMES MARSHALL

"All this violence," said my mom. "What are my friends going to think?"

"Back in my day, if you decapitated your parents, people looked at you like you were *weird*," said my dad.

Perhaps I should've gone with a sword, for ease of use and relative cleanliness, but I find, and this is just my personal experience, maybe you've had different results, but I find nothing beats the hatchet when your goal is the spectacle kill, because it's smaller and lighter than the axe, yet it retains that menacing look, and furthermore, its reduced size brings you closer to your victim or, if it's your parents, your victimizers, because ultimately, your parents are your murderers.

"I like your hatchet," said my dad.

"Really? I just got it." I held it closer to him. "I don't know if you noticed this little detail right here but . . . hey . . . wait a minute. Yeah, nice try, Dad."

After I severed my parents' heads, and Mrs. Burnett's, so they'd starve to death and die again, or at least not actively live undead anymore, I decided I couldn't leave them like that, so I cut their doctrinally rigid, covered-in-closed-minded-wounds-that-never-bleed, not-sorry-sores-that-never-weep, gross, pale grey bodies into little pieces, and then I destroyed their mindless minds—it was sort of a mincing action—and to put an exclamation mark on the whole monstrous matter, I doused their inflexible, bloodless pieces, and when I say "bloodless" I mean "emotionless" because their pieces were, in point of fact, actually very bloody, which was awesome; blood is awesome, everybody knows that; and anyway, in addition to all the parts of my parents and my English teacher, I doused the house—my childhood home—in premium gasoline, lit it, and walked outside, casually, letting the dripping hatchet hang down by my side, bad-ass style, and then I turned back to watch, remorselessly, while my past strained uselessly toward the sky in a magic orange-yellow shape, and, shortly thereafter, I uploaded video of the entire event to my website: HowToEndHumanSuffering.com.

I don't know if it happens every time, but sometimes when you kill your parents with a hatchet, a centaur appears to you. That's what happened to me. He had the upper half of a man and the body of a horse. His upper half, the man half, was shirtless and muscular. His lower half, the horse half, was palomino: golden-tan.

"Guy Boy Man," he said, bowing down to me. "My name is Centaur111." He straightened up. "I've come from Fairyland to accompany you on a series of exciting adventures."

"I always thought Fairyland was a mythical place, like Nirvana, Shangri-La, or Funkytown," I said.

"Fairyland is real and some of our exciting adventures will take us there," he said. "Right now a lot of beautiful female fairies, pixies, nymphs, and sprites want to spend some serious quality time with you there; everybody is buzzing about the stand you're taking against the undead. We, the supernatural creatures, have been forced into an uneasy alliance with zombies. We rebuild what they tear down so the cycle of creation and destruction can continue."

"If supernatural creatures partner with zombies, then supernatural creatures are my enemy too."

"One thing at a time, Guy Boy Man. Before you declare war on me and my kind, first enjoy the pleasures of female fairies, pixies, nymphs, and sprites."

"Yeah, I can do that," I said.

"And then let's go on a series of exciting adventures," said Centaur111. "They will prepare you for your struggle with the zombies and those that control them. And when we get back, I'll help you attain unimaginable wealth in exchange for one simple promise."

"What's the promise?" I asked.

"In exchange for trillions and trillions of American dollars, you can never tell a human female you love her. If you do, you lose your money."

"Why can't I just have the money without any conditions?" I asked.

"That's just how it is," said Centaur111.

It sounded okay to me. I mean, I'd never been in love before. And I couldn't see myself experiencing that for the first time in the near future so it didn't really seem like a huge ask. It wasn't like I had a girlfriend or anything. I didn't know how hard it could be to go without saying those three little words. "I guess you've got a deal," I said.

"Ride me, Guy Boy Man," said Centaur111.

I just stood there for a minute. Without moving my head, I looked from side to side. Then I climbed onto Centaur111's back and we set off.

After I had all kinds of good times with female fairies, pixies, nymphs, and sprites—the details of which I won't go into here; talk to me later—and after I went on a series of exciting adventures I can't be bothered to relate here, Centaur111 was beside me as I stood in front of the ATM.

"Remember," said Centaur111. "In exchange for this money, you can never tell a girl you love her. If you do, you lose all your money."

"I remember," I said.

The ATM asked me how much I wanted to withdraw. I hit the "Completely" button.

Now I have so much money it's obscene. Recently the zombie Supreme Court ruled that money is speech. That's typical zombie mindlessness. It's like ruling that water is cross country skis. Obviously, it's not. But if money is speech, then I have the most say in the world. (And the poor are silent. Which sucks for them.)

Anyway, it turns out it's really hard to wipe zombies off the face of the planet and tear down all their mindless institutions, especially when you're drunk and partying with hot young girls all the time, so I decided to start small: I resolved to clean up my high school.

Here at Scare City High School, the occasional drop of total darkness, interspersed with stroboscopic sights from the flickering lights, combined with the constant presence of electricity and water in close proximity (i.e., the leaking pipes and exposed wires), like in our brains, lends an (oxygen-less) air of terror to the hallways.

Leaning back against my locker, I take another swig of whiskey, savouring the holy fire in my throat and mind. I'm wearing a ceremonial robe. It's made of shiny, white, high-tech-plastic; it's divided in the front, but it seals there seamlessly. Additionally, I'm wearing a pirate hat. It's the Pope's hat: the big tall golden one. I had it pirated. Now it's mine. Completing my look, and juxtaposed against my shiny white robe, is my glossy-dark-feathered faithful shoulder-perched bird that never craps on me like my parents did.

"Hey, Guy Boy Man," someone calls out. "I like your black parrot!"

"It's a raven," I call back. "Get it right. But thanks."

I basically pirated all my money from the global economy, and, in order to lead others out of despair, I became a spiritual leader, and all spiritual leaders are basically pirates, taking power and giving nothing in return, so now I consider myself, and encourage all others to consider me, a pirate. (The details of my religion can be found on HowToEndHumanSuffering.com; it's basically a violent, individualistic form of Christianity.)

When I was searching for the best shoulder-perched bird, I briefly considered the pirate's traditional companion: the parrot. I quickly discarded this idea because I don't want some stupid squawker reciting a list of all my secrets at some inopportune time. Then I considered the most bad-ass bird: the bald eagle. (America!) It turns out this is the mistake most pirates make; hence the eye-patch. Finally, I decided on the raven. Firstly, the raven is always ready to feast on the dead bodies of my enemies, which I appreciate. Secondly, goth girls dig it, which is cool.

The ghost of my parents' voices haunts me. My father criticizes: "Back in my day, we didn't have time for birds. We had to get to *work*." My mother worries: "You're wearing a ceremonial robe! What are my friends going to think?" My father grabs me: "Back in my day, if you walked around in a stupid hat like that, people looked at you like you were *weird*." I shake my head, trying to get rid of them.

Here's something you might not know just from looking at me: I'm very attractive. I'm not good-looking or anything. I'm skinny. I'm pale. My eyes are sunken and circled by dark rings. (I've always been engaged to the inside and kept awake by its night.) And my thick black hair is in constant revolt, never lying down. (No matter how often I go to the salon, my thick black hair is always too long to be short, and too short to be long.) No. I'm attractive because I'm powerful; I'm powerful because I'm wealthy; and I'm confident because I'm both.

Walking in the hallway, zombie teenagers stare at me warily, and, I have to admit, scarily. I'm the only one who can see them for what they are, and they know it. Their outstretched arms are bound at the wrists with grey rope.

N V P F Z

Their open mouths (full of blue tongues and broken but still sharp teeth) are muzzled behind shiny stainless steel face cages. They still disturb me. They're no threat to me, physically, bound as they are now, but they do something to my mind. I want to get away from them. I want *them* to get away from *me*. Looking at them, I shudder. I shudder to think. I take another drink.

I try to focus on the (few) living kids going by. Mostly the hot young girls. They pick their way over the brokenness and try not to slip on the slickness. Slim girls, slender girls, thin girls. I look at them all. I don't discriminate. As I watch the flashing, artificial-light girls in the hallway, random voices divide the living murmurs and the moans of the undead, the shuffling zombie feet and the alive kids' squeaking sneakers, and call out to me, "Hey, Guy Boy Man, your religion is better than all the others put together, including science!" and "Your religion saved my useless and worthless life, Guy Boy Man!"

I hold up my whiskey bottle at the youth of America. "Good morning, idiots," I say, in a toast. I take another swig.

The main goal of my religion is to have a really great time; adjunctive to that goal is my plight to end all human suffering, mostly through ending all human reproduction (right now any idiot can breed, and, sadly, most idiots do). When human reproduction has ceased, or been drastically reduced, we'll decrease, perhaps even eliminate, the zombie food supply. I readily admit my objective is ambitious. Humans have been reproducing for a long time. But it's good to set goals.

Since I probably won't be able to stop people from reproducing within my target timeline—six to eight weeks—I've set myself a more manageable goal: to stop the One responsible for the horrific state of Scare City High

School and for all the terrifying things that happen here.

Suddenly, a zombie girl turns and walks straight into the locker next to mine. She bounces off it. (All the zombie teenagers are forced, by their zombie parents, to wear helmets at all times to avoid accidentally bashing out their own brains.) The zombie girl backs up a bit and walks into the locker next to mine again. She stumbles back again. She seems to think she should be able to get through it. Actually, no. It seems like she doesn't think at all. It also seems like she doesn't recognize negative stimuli. I don't know, though. Maybe she's attempting to align all the empty spaces in her body with all the empty spaces in the locker so she can pass through it into a classroom. Or maybe there's supposed to be some sort of zombie portal at the locker next to mine. (I think I'm really giving her the benefit of the doubt with those last two.)

Every time she walks into the locker, her hands, which are tied together, clang into the locker first, and are forced up over her helmeted head as she continues forward without paying attention to her outstretched arms. She's wearing a ragged, knee-length, black skirt and a grey T-shirt that's splotched purple with blood stains. She's also wearing heavily scuffed white high heels. One of the shoes challenges the definition of "high heel" because it no longer has a heel; it's, like, a "low heel," or a "non-high, non-heel," or a "messy white flat" or something; (the word "white" is probably misplaced too.) From under her battered black helmet, the zombie girl's dirty red hair sticks out and hangs in impossible ways, held in place by garbage goo and the scum of scum. She walks into the locker again. I push-kick her in the hip, moving her a few zombie steps to the side. She turns and stares at me with her lifeless white eyes. A (manly) chill runs up my spine. I look at the shiny stainless steel cage covering her mouth. Those thin bars arranged horizontally and curved up and back to meet just above her ears where they curve over and down—spreading into another array of stainless steel bars behind her head, holding the muzzle in place under the back of her helmet— are my only protection from her bite, and from sharing her pointless plight. "Get out of here, zombie chick!" I hiss. She doesn't understand, and it's obvious, but, luckily, she stumbles away, so it doesn't matter.

Teenagers keep passing me in the hallway. They don't go anywhere. They just keep passing. They're nameless. Faceless. They're zombies. Even the ones that aren't zombies. They just aren't zombies *yet*. The ones that won't become zombies are doomed to be zombie food. God. I hate high school.

The kids aren't the only life-(and non-life)-forms in the hallway. There's something greenish-brown on all the water fountains. I *think* they're water fountains. The water has never been tested, as far as I know. If I sound paranoid, it's because there's a very real chance someone is trying to kill us so they don't have to neglect us anymore. Anyway, the greenish-brown life-form is making pretty good progress up the walls. Our biology teacher says it's God's will. I assume the musty smell is God's will too.

As you know, I've taken it upon myself—I've also taken it upon a bunch of other people who will actually do the hard work—to stop the One who's to blame for all the terrifying things that happen at Scare City High School; the One who's responsible for the horrific state of everything. Who is he? (Not that he couldn't be a she.) Who's accountable for all this? He's a mystery: unknown and unknowable. Yet we here at Scare City High exist according to his pronouncements. A figureless shadow, he rewards the good, punishes the bad, and decides which is which or just always knows. He is my enemy. I've never seen him, personally, but I've met a few who swear they have. I've shaken their shoulders. I've seen the fear in their wide eyes. "Where is he?" I've cried. "Where is he?"

He's in the broken glass threatening to cut us. He's in the mould slowly poisoning us. He's in the leaking plumbing and backed-up toilets and graffiti. He's in the warping and staining and rot. He's everywhere and we are not. Does he have a name? No. He has a title.

The Principal.

And I, Guy Boy Man, will end his reign of terror.

Or I'll guide the people who will end his reign of terror. Usually I like to act in a supervisory capacity.

In my head, my dad says, "Back in my day, we didn't have time to end reigns of terror. We had to get to *work*."

As if to cleanse my palate from my encounter with the zombie chick who kept walking into the locker next to mine, a cute girl with pink hair emerges from the hallway's flashing filth and gloom. The cute girl's pink hair is straight, slightly longer than shoulder length, and twice divided: once at her centre part; again at the tops of her shoulders. Some of it falls in front of her; some of it behind. Her flawless skin is breast-milk-white.

She walks right up to me. A glowing white unicorn struts beside her. Its hooves click silently on the hallway floor. I didn't know hooves could click silently, but apparently they can. With unicorns. In any event, the girl and the unicorn stop directly in front of me. Lowering her head a little, meekly, the cute girl brushes hair back behind her ears with her fingertips, looking at me the whole time. Her eyes are the most amazing colour I've never seen before. The grey of them is so light it's almost white. She looks dead.

N V P F Z

Not undead. When she looks at me, she looks *peacefully* dead. All I see is white, absence, the lack of black, nothing holy, just nothing, and I think it's all the more beautiful for just being the product of chance, of the unspeakable, unimaginable number of possibilities that were tried and rejected before we both somehow ended up right here, at this exact moment, which is, of course, magical and, arguably, holy, in how mind-bogglingly fortuitous it is, if you're a fan of suffering, which I, personally, am not, and if you believe this, all of this, life (or whatever it is) is real, truly real, happening once and only once, exactly as it seems, tangibly, substantially, and that other people are actually experiencing it in the same way, which I, personally, don't.

If they did, they would've fixed it, right?

At my school, in addition to the greenish-brown "life-form" growing on and from what we believe (we're supposed to think) are water fountains, there's also a blackish-red substance splashed and splattered over all the lockers on both sides of the hallway. Some think it's dried blood. Others aren't so sure. Most of us are pretty convinced, though.

Suddenly the cute girl turns cautious. She glances side to side, making sure no one is watching. Then she leans close, lifts her chin at me, and says, conspiratorially, "You're Guy Boy Man, right?"

I squint at her, suspicious. "You a cop?"

"No." She leans back, stunned. "I'm a regular girl with pink hair and a unicorn."

I nod, still squinting at her. "Maybe that's your cover."

She's wearing four-inch shiny black stilettos, very skinny dark blue jeans, and a tight, white man's dress shirt. It isn't a "white man's dress shirt," per se. Obviously, men of different ethnicities could wear it. Anyway, this cute girl looks great in the shirt I'm talking about, which isn't tucked in, but isn't long enough to cover her ass in case I want to take a look later, which I will, just so you know. The sleeves are rolled up just below her elbows. The top three buttons are undone, showing off the tops of her big breasts and a bit of her lacy red bra. I didn't mention she had big breasts earlier because that sort of thing isn't polite to notice right away, even though I totally noticed it right away. I even noticed how the two pieces of her divided shirt are brought together and held in place by phallic buttons pushed through vaginal holes, and I noted the way the fabric is stretched in taut ripples over her breasts like a textbook picture of (dissatisfied) cells dividing.

"Cops pretend to be cute fifteen-year-old girls all the time," I point out.

The unicorn has its majestic head turned toward the girl. It's looking at me, nobly, not threateningly, but with complete confidence, from one of its dark eyes. (I'm not too surprised to see a unicorn; unicorns are mentioned six times in the King James Version of the Bible; I believe in a strict literal interpretation of pretty much everything; doesn't everybody?)

The girl shrugs. She's wearing a pearl necklace, and a thin gold chain that carries a small gold cross. (I don't use the word "jewellery" because I'm not anti-Semitic.) I think about the nature of the decorative circles around her neck. I think about the divided beginning and end. I think about the clasps. Her skin is so white, the tight string of pearls around her neck looks darker in comparison. She isn't wearing makeup, but her lips are almost blue, like she's hypothermic. "I'm not a cop," she insists.

"Well I'm going to tell the judge you said so." I take a slug of whiskey. "Obviously, the judge won't care, because he'll be out to get me, but I'm going to tell him anyway, just so it's on the record, and then, someday, historians can write about how unfairly everybody treated me!" I guzzle a few more shots and set the bottle down on the floor, next to my backpack. I turn away from the girl. "I didn't mean to imply the judge couldn't be a woman." I grab my cigarettes and lighter from the top shelf of my locker. When I turn back, I offer the cute girl a butt, but she just shakes her head. "So what do you want, cop?" I spark a cigarette and blow smoke up at the broken ceiling. "If this is in regards to my big cock fighting ring, I don't know what the hell you're talking about."

No one knows exactly *when* the school started falling apart. It's unclear whether anyone tried to maintain it after it was built—if those who built the school gave up sometime during construction, or if the materials themselves were just never really that into it. I guess it's all about how close you want to look or how far back you want to go. I'm not sure there's a difference.

"It's not about your big cock fighting ring." Turning away, the pink-haired girl reaches over, puts her hand on the unicorn, and pats its back a couple of times. It seems like a gesture more to comfort her than the unicorn.

"Sure." I nod at her, unconvinced. She's slender but not skinny. There's a softness to her. Looking at her, I feel like if I grabbed her arms, I'd grab something, something real, but I've been wrong before. "Do you like hardcore pornography?"

"Of course not." She says it like it's a ridiculous question.

"How come?"

"It degrades women."

"It degrades men too. It degrades everybody *equally*."

"Whatever," she says. "It's disgusting."

"My dad used to say that back in his day, you couldn't get hardcore pornography, day or night, without leaving the comfort of your own home," I tell her. "You had to buy it from a guy in a brick-and-mortar store. And he looked at you like you were weird."

"Really?" she asks, trying not to look at my robe, trying to think of something else to see. She reaches out to her unicorn again.

"Yeah." I take a drag off my smoke. "So what are you going to pretend you want to talk about when you really want to talk about my big cock fighting ring?"

Most of the (few) students who (can be bothered to) think about where everything went wrong with the school (usually) point to the ill-qualified, faint-hearted, namby-pamby, liberal administration's (surprisingly principled) decision to stand up to the corporate interests providing so much of the school's funding. You see, in exchange for millions of dollars that went toward the school's operating budget, these corporate interests—almost entirely junk food and caffeinated sugar drink vendors—were allowed to advertise in the school's hallways, cafeteria, and (ironically) gymnasium. They were permitted to place vending machines near every entrance and exit. Along with every middle area. One day (it might have been around the time we had to bring in bigger desks and chairs for some of our "more loveable" schoolmates), the administration decided it might *not* be in the (ballooning) student body's best interests to have such easy access to unhealthy food and drink. To be fair, some of the (few) students who (can be bothered to) think about where everything went wrong *also* point to the *lack* of funding that *necessitated* the acceptance of corporate funding in the first place.

Stroking the unicorn's side, and looking, lovingly, at

the white beast that glows on its own, the girl says, "I want to ask you for a favour."

"Is it a sexual favour?" I say.

"Yes."

"I'm listening."

I can smell her perfume. It's intoxicating. Maybe that's the whiskey. The cute girl definitely has a scent, though. She smells familiar. Familiar but exotic. It takes me a moment to place her bouquet in the vase of my brain and identify the flowers. She smells like baby oil.

Suddenly, she looks flustered. She lets her hand slip off the unicorn. She turns to me. "I'm a . . ."—her pale face flushes, taking on the pink hue of her hair—". . . I don't want to say the word." She squeezes her eyes shut and shakes her head a little. Her swinging hair catches the flickering fluorescence in waves: in bright peaks and dark troughs. Her cotton-candy-pink hair isn't washed out red. It's true pink: soft and light but deep and lush; it's somehow almost silvery. The cute girl opens her heavenly grey eyes, and stares at me, determined. "I've never had . . ."—she stops herself again, and her shoulders fall, and she tilts one of her high heels over to the side, and looks down at it—". . . okay I don't want to say that word, either."

"This is probably going to take a long time if you discriminate against words, which you should never do. Discriminating against words is wrong." I take a drag off my cigarette, exhale, and tap ashes on the hallway floor. "Except for nigger."

She sighs. "What I'm trying to say is, you're a bad boy."

I look at my cigarette. At first blush, it's a white tube filled with brown tobacco. Then I stick it between my lips and watch the tip of it burn orange while I suck on it and marvel, slightly cross-eyed, at how the colour becomes a part of me, how it moves with me, my breath, my intake of air, purified by the fire, and then (admittedly) it becomes *less* purified by the tobacco and carcinogenic chemicals and anyway the pretty orange colour crackles, if a colour can crackle, through the brown and the white, toward me, when I suck, and believe me, I suck. I suck non-stop. I'm going to die from sucking but everybody dies from sucking and ultimately so will the world. I take a deep drag, trap the cigarette in a scissor-closing peace sign, take it out from between my lips, and exhale smoke at the fallen ceiling. I stick the cigarette back between my lips and let it dangle. I look really cool when I do that. "Kike," I say.

"What?"

"It's okay to discriminate against the word 'kike.' "

"I suppose that's okay. I don't really." She tries to compose herself. "Like I was saying, you're a bad boy."

"Yeah well . . . 'Faggot, dyke' . . . I'm a spiritual leader and a pirate. Being a bad boy kind of goes with the territory, which I control and rule with an iron fist."

"Right," she says. "You're a bad boy and I'm a good girl. So I thought you could help me out."

"Help you out how?"

"Look," says the cute girl, exasperated. "I want you to have sex with me. I've never done it before."

"Did you know that one in five Americans has genital warts?" I say, seriously.

"No," she says, taken aback. "Wow. That's a startling statistic." She frowns at me. "Why? Do you have genital warts?"

I don't answer right away. Then I say, "No, but if I did, I wouldn't be alone."

"Right." Even more exasperated, the cute girl slaps

her hands onto her face. She drags them down slowly, seemingly trying to pull off her skin, but only stretching it, and drawing down her lower eyelids, exposing the moist pink surrounding the important beauty of her eyes. "Listen . . ."

The blue hallway suddenly goes black. Someone screams. Animals shriek and batter the insides of lockers in answer.

"What's that noise?" asks the cute girl, bathed in unicorn light, her head turned in the direction of the shrieking animals.

"It's not the sound of excited cocks," I say, defensively. I want to change the topic. "What's your name, cute girl?"

"Baby Doll15."

The fluorescent lights glimmer back on. Not all of them. A lot of the fluorescent lights are broken. Their sharp white pieces are mixed in the debris of broken light-grey ceiling tiles. "Well, Baby Doll15, if you're going to get involved with me, I think you should know I have my demons." I gesture with my thumb over my left shoulder. "That's Mike Hawk." I point my thumb over my right shoulder. "That's York Hunt." My demons seem to appear as I acknowledge them.

"What's up?" say Mike and York in unison, with their mouths full, lifting their Hot Pockets as if to say, "Cheers." In their non-Hot-Pocket-holding hands, they've got Red Bulls.

"Only two?" says Baby Doll15. "I'm impressed."

"Actually they're more like elected representatives of all my other demons."

"I see." That's what she says, but I don't know if it's true.

It gets awkward. I feel like she wants to tell me about her demons, or her angels, but instead, the two of us just stand there, looking at each other. Every once in a while, I steal a glance at the unicorn. It's a pretty awesome unicorn.

"Is that your unicorn?" I finally ask.

"It's not mine. It just follows me around."

"Have you ever tried to kill it?" I say. "Ride it, I mean."

"No."

I take a swig of my whiskey. It tastes like love and acceptance. "Okay, yeah, I think I can help you. I mean, I regularly bring girls to heights of sexual frustration they've never even contemplated, let alone experienced, and as soon as I'm done, I abruptly end the encounter and make them feel like their presence is no longer wanted. I think that's what you're looking for." I wipe my lips with the back of my hand. Then I suck on my cigarette and inhale it so deep that when I breathe out, no smoke appears. It tastes like the future.

"Okay," she says, uncomfortable, "so can I come over after school and we can get it over with or what?"

"Not that I'm complaining or anything, but why are you in such a hurry to do this?"

She looks up and sighs. "I'm sick of it, you know? I'm sick of *having* it. I'm sick of *being* it. I'm sick of *thinking* about it, *wondering* about it, and *worrying* about it. I'm sick of *wanting* it, quite a bit sometimes, but *being afraid* of it, and I'm sick of wanting it to be perfect and *knowing* it never will be. I just want to get rid of it so I can get on with my life."

"All right. Fair enough. Why me?"

"Because I know you won't care. I'll just be another one to you. A number you can add to your list. I don't want any complications."

"Do it," says one of my demons, Mike Hawk, with his mouth full of Hot Pocket, taking a drink of Red Bull.

"Oh for sure," agrees York Hunt, chewing and smiling.

N V P F Z

Their encouragement is worrisome. Acknowledging your demons and paying close attention to them is a good idea because demons actually make the most trustworthy advisors, inasmuch as whatever they suggest is a really bad idea. You can always count on them; you can completely rely on them. You can't listen to the angels because angels are constantly trying to pass off really unpleasant tests, tasks, and trials as something you should eagerly accept just because God wants you to. Screw that. Wander around in the desert? Get crucified? Not me, God. You do it.

"So do you want to get together after school or what?" Baby Doll15 asks, getting impatient.

"Not right after school. I've got to strategize after school. You know. Arrange some preparations, prepare some arrangements. I'm getting set to remove The Principal from office. Maybe tonight."

"Text me?"

"Argh."

She turns and walks away. I take a good long look at her ass as she goes. It's nice and tight. That's the way I like my girls' asses: nice and tight. The unicorn clicks into silent step behind her, obscuring my view of that ass.

Stupid unicorn.

CHAPTER TWO:
Enter Sweetie Honey; Not Literally; Okay, Literally, But Not Like That

After Baby Doll15 and her unicorn disappear into the stroboscopic crowd of students, I decide I'd better get ready for class. I move my pirate hat—the Pope's pirate hat: the tall gold-and-white one—back and forth on my head, adjusting it. My raven bounces on my shoulder a few times, trying to decide if it should take flight, but it doesn't. I take one last drag off my smoke, flick it away, and turn to my locker. I pull out two nine-millimetre handguns, make sure they're loaded and there's one in the chamber so I'm ready for that troubled kid to, invariably, show up and start shooting up the school. After I make sure the safeties are on, I stick the guns into the mirror-image holsters I have strapped to my lower back. Along with the holsters, underneath my ceremonial robe, I'm *also* wearing my pirate outfit: a pair of brown breeches and a loose-fitting white linen shirt.

It happens impossibly fast: between flicks of fluorescent lights. One millisecond he isn't there; the next he is. Some guy I've never seen before is working on the combination lock on the locker right next to mine: the one the zombie chick kept walking into. He's wearing spotless white sneakers, casual-fit blue jeans, and a tight dark red t-shirt, revealing his trim but muscular chest, shoulders, and arms.

"You a cop?" I ask, squinting at him coldly.

"Ninja," he says.

I eye him suspiciously. "Maybe that's your cover."

"My cover is that I'm a regular kid."

"But you're really a ninja."

"Exactly." He pops the combination lock.

"Okay, that's pretty cool," I admit, nodding. "I'm a pirate."

"Nice."

The (well-known) rivalry between ninjas and pirates is (mostly) friendly. Normally I'm not really an exclamation mark kind of guy, but I'm pretty enthusiastic about being a pirate! I get all my music, movies, and software for free! (No, not like a communist. Well, okay, kind of like a communist, but in an awesome way.) Without doubt, we pirates are the coolest! We fly the skull and crossbones! It's unquestionably the wickedest flag of all time! (Did you know "ninja" is the plural of "ninja"?) [That's scary. I've got to admit it. (They don't use the "s" because it'd slow them down and make it harder for them to hide when guards are nearby.)] (But I don't abide by the no "s" rule. I think it discriminates against blind people. It's like with deer. If you're with a blind person and you say, "Hey, look at the deer!" the blind person doesn't know how many deer you're talking about. There could be one deer, or there could be a lot of deer. There might not be any deer at all and you could be messing with the blind person. I'm just saying. When I'm talking about more than one ninja, I say "ninjas," because of blind people.) Ninjas don't have a flag! If they did, it'd have to be a completely invisible flag because of their insatiable secrecy-lust, but they don't, because they're not awesome enough, but I have to admit I can't *conclusively* say ninjas don't have a flag because if they *do* have an invisible flag, obviously, I wouldn't know it, even if it was slapping me in the face. I mean, I'd know something invisible and fabric-like was slapping me in the face, but I wouldn't know it was an invisible ninja flag. (I could probably deduce it was.) I also have to acknowledge that an invisible flag, no matter what image, motto, or lack thereof should be sewn into it, or left off of it, would be very impressive. It might even rival the skull and crossbones. She'd certainly be an ominous non-warning to all who never see her! Not that all flags are chicks. Whatever. We pirates have ships! Ninjas don't. Unless they have ships nobody can see.

Okay, okay. Even though I'm a pirate and proud of it, I've got to give the edge to ninjas in a head to head match-up. But that's mostly on the grounds of intimidation. There are other things to consider. Quality of life, for example. Furthermore, I'm not *just* a pirate. I'm the Self-Appointed One. No one can make you the "Self-Appointed One." This is America. You've got to do things yourself. Unless you've got Mexicans.

I crouch down, pick up my half-empty bottle of whiskey, and take a swig. Pirates are supposed to drink rum, but I don't. That's how bad-ass I am. I look at what's left in the bottle. It's half-empty. I drank what's missing. Cause and effect. I've got to live with the consequences of my actions [even if my actions are beyond my control because of genetic predispositions, my formative years, and the situations into which I've been forced without my consent, including (but not limited to) the world, everything in it, on it, around it, and myself. Furthermore (unfortunately), I've also got to live with the (horrific) consequences of everyone else's (idiotic) actions, even if their (stupid) actions are beyond their control too.] That's why I drink heavily. Maybe I'm half-empty, as well. Whatever.

Suddenly a girl floats past me and the ninja, down the hallway. I don't mean she passes in a way that makes her look light on her feet. I mean she literally *floats* by us. She's about a yard off the slippery, rubble-strewn floor. Her arms are stretched out to the sides. Her feet are bare. Her legs are straight and held together tightly. It looks like she's being carried, but no one is carrying her. Wildly, panicked, the girl jerks her head from side to side, searching for the cause of her predicament.

Some say Scare City High is haunted by the wasted potential of all those who are trained to become zombies. Others agree.

The poor girl wears a long white silk dress that's pressed tight against her front, like it's being blown back by a strong wind, revealing every bump, line, and curve of her thin body. The diaphanous fabric flows in rapidly undulating waves behind her. Her long blonde hair flows behind her too, blown by the same wind I can't feel. In the flashing blue-white light, the floating girl is a little eerie. She's being followed by a bunch of kids holding up their cell phones, recording her. The kids are open-mouthed but silent.

"I've got my ninja outfit in my backpack," says the ninja, ignoring the floating girl and the crowd passing behind him. He turns to me, leaving the open combination lock dangling from his locker. "I'm not wearing it right now because I just transferred to this school, and I really want to fit in. Thankfully, I have my male-model-rugged-good-looks and my easy-going charm, not to mention my mastery-of-various-fighting-styles and weapons, to help."

"All of that will come in handy," I agree. "Here, and, you know"—I gesture with the whiskey bottle in a way that very precisely indicates I'm talking about the future—"when you enter the workforce."

A little ways down the hall, the floating girl gets pinned with her arms outspread, halfway up a wall. Nothing happens for a moment. Then she gets pulled away from the wall by the same invisible force holding her aloft. She gets slammed back into the wall. She screams in pain and terror. The kids documenting everything on their cell phones gasp. The floating girl gets pulled away again and slammed back again. She shakes her head from side to side impossibly fast, screaming at the top of her lungs. The witnesses call for more witnesses.

"People are reluctant to befriend ninjas," says the ninja, sadly, to me, "especially when they're dressed up like ninjas. It's a tragedy. Ninjas need love, you know? Well, we don't need it. We could live alone in a cave if we had to. Or by ourselves on a mountain, if we wanted to. Ninjas don't *need* anything. Other than our wits. One free finger. That sort of thing. We simply don't, due to our training and our ways, require the sort of stuff regular people do. But that doesn't mean we don't *want* it. I guess what I'm trying to say is, aside from our ability to move stealthily, or, when necessary, remain completely still, and, ultimately, our gift—because it's a gift, really, that's what my father says, and I agree—our gift for, remorselessly killing lots and lots of people in a variety of different ways—which would be too long to list here—we're just like regular people. Regular people who aren't merely pretending to be regular people, I mean."

I guzzle from the bottle. I set it on the floor. "I hear you." I reach into my locker, pull out a pump-action sawed-off shotgun, and pump it once. An unused shell flies out. I forgot I'd pumped it already. I retrieve the shell and reload it. I've got the sawed-off shotgun, in addition to the nine-millimetres, so I'm ready for when *a group* of troubled kids shows up and starts shooting up the school. Sawed-off shotguns are good for crowds of people, and when I say, "good," I mean, "bad." The shotgun has a strap. I sling it over my shoulder.

The ninja turns away from me, opens his locker, and hangs the lock on the inside of the door. The inside of the door is plastered with pictures of shirtless dudes. They're really hunky-looking shirtless dudes.

Down the hall, more kids are gathering, watching the girl being tortured by the unknown. Invisible hands ruffle her white silk gown. They touch her everywhere. They do things to her. Various, you know, things. Use your imagination. I notice a couple of guys exchange smiles, keeping their cell phones on the action. The girl's head and her long blonde hair hang slackly. She's unconscious or she's surrendered.

Drawn to the meat—the confusion and fear—muzzled and bound zombie teenagers join the crowd of spectators. They don't look at the tortured girl. With their glazed white eyes, in their mottled grey faces, they stare down the hall at me.

The ninja scopes out the swords and throwing stars neatly arranged inside his locker. "You expecting trouble?" he asks me bravely and, I've got to say, handsomely, tipping his head in the direction of the shotgun I just slung over my shoulder.

"Always."

"What kind of trouble?"

"Big."

"You're a dude and I like that," says the ninja.

I squint at him.

"You're a dude who lives by a code and I like that," says the ninja. "That's what I meant to say."

"Okay." I look back at the inside of the ninja's locker door, plastered with pictures of shirtless dudes. Like I said before, they're really hunky-looking shirtless dudes. I don't think I mentioned this earlier: their chests are very shiny.

"I've got my ninja outfit in my backpack."

"That's what you said."

"I mean. When there's trouble. If you need a hand or anything."

"Thanks. I'm heavily armed right now, so I think I'm good, which is actually a pretty deep comment."

"Gotcha."

All of a sudden the girl down the hall starts screaming again. This time she screams louder and at a higher frequency, like what's happening to her now is the worst so far, and the worst she can possibly survive. I don't know what's more startling: the scream or when it stops. Abruptly. Her head hangs again. This time her long blonde hair doesn't. It, along with her white silk gown, gets blown to the side by a strong but unfelt wind.

The ninja finally acknowledges the girl's miserable existence. "What's her problem?" He jerks his thumb over his shoulder.

"She's being tortured by the unknown."

"Does that happen a lot around here?"

"Yeah. This is Scare City High. You're new so you don't know. This place is pretty much a horror movie. I've managed to learn everything that happens here is because of a shadowy figure called The Principal. He wants us all to become zombies or zombie food. Basically, I'm searching for him with an eye toward destroying him. It's no big deal. Hey. Can I ask you something about black guys?"

I realize that sounds like a random question, but the handsome, strong-looking ninja is black. Actually, his skin is more like a beautiful golden-brown colour. It's either from a lack of something or an abundance of something; I can't remember which, what, or if I ever knew. [Interesting tidbit, ninjas don't wear black outfits; they wear dark red, white, or blue; get it straight, Hollywood. (White can be dark too, especially in snow shadows.)] I just didn't mention the attractive, physically intimidating ninja is black, or golden brown, earlier, because I'm so tolerant.

"What do you want to know about black guys?" asks the ninja. "Is it the penis thing?"

"No," I say, making a face like, *that's ridiculous.*

The hallway goes dark. For a moment, the only light to be seen, or seen by, is the open cell phones down the hall, mechanically struggling to witness the girl's torment in the gloom. Then the tube-shaped artificial suns hanging over us precariously in their rectangular metal boxes dangling from wires not meant to bear this kind of weight—wrapped tightly around each other, like lovers' legs—begin to flicker again.

The ninja's hair, cropped brutally closely, is merciless shades of brown darker than his skin. "Is it the rhythm thing?"

"No."

"The athletic thing?" The ninja's closely cropped hair is sculpted, heartlessly; never moving, or always moving unobserved, and silently, it flows in ruthless curves and viciously straight lines. "The short temper thing? The absentee father thing?"

"It was the penis thing," I confess.

"I don't know about all black guys," says the ninja, nodding, like he thought so, "but I have an enormous penis."

"That's great," I say, sincerely, lifting my bottle to him.

"Seriously. Congratulations."

"Thanks. Hey." He points at me. "You want to see it?" He starts undoing his jeans.

"Yes and no."

Before I know it, I'm gawking at what can only be described as a long, thick, milk-chocolate brown serpent; some kind of giant whacked-out treat you'd get if Easter was way different.

"All men were *not* created equal," I say, staring at the ninja's huge penis.

"It's kind of a waste," he says, shrugging, putting it away. "I can't use very much of it without hurting . . . people."

It occurs to me now that I shouldn't refer to the ninja as black or golden brown. I should refer to him as African-American. I hate that, though. Aren't we all African-Americans? I mean, when you get right down to it? Obviously, people who aren't American aren't African-Americans, but they wish they were. American. They probably don't wish they were black, if they're white. Because of discrimination. Racism. That's wrong, though. Black people are white people too! Seriously. They're close enough. We should start saying so. It's going to be awkward with the really dark ones but we'll get used to it.

The stroboscopic girl suffering at the hands of the unknown is now dangling face-down in mid-air! It seems she's being held up by her splayed arms and legs; they're higher than the rest of her body. Her white silk gown and her long blonde hair are being buffeted downwards by a wind from above. One male teenager holds his up his cell phone and jumps, taking pictures of her ass. The girl isn't screaming anymore. A small but discernible vibration courses through her thin body. A space opens below her.

The ninja's backpack is slung over one shoulder; his thumb is under the strap. He directs my attention behind my back and says, "Four exotically beautiful Eastern European girls down there are staring at my muscular chest, shoulders, arms, and my I've-been-told-repeatedly-by-a-large-number-of-people really cute butt."

"Right on."

"Quick word about my naked body," he says. "Amazing."

I don't really know what to say to that, so I say, "Okay."

All of a sudden, the suspended girl starts falling. It happens outside of regular time. I see it as a slow, peaceful descent but I know it's a brutal, violent event for her. Her hands and feet, which were higher than her body, are now lower than her body. They're being pulled toward the floor faster than her body can fall. She's not being dropped; she's being yanked straight down. Her long blonde hair and white silk gown, which had been oriented downwards, now shoot upwards while she descends so painfully slowly. I want to scream. In my fear for her. I want to yell. For someone to catch her. But it all happens too slowly.

She mashes into the floor. Her flesh flows out in waves that would crash and splash if not for her skin. Her ribcage compresses visibly; it cracks audibly. Her legs and arms, which hit the ground first, are already airborne again in their upward bounce. They reach their apex and are restrained by biology and physics when her anguished head hits rock bottom, cracks open, and spills shades of grey.

My demons, Mike Hawk and York Hunt, are suddenly standing next to the ninja and me. They're eating Hot Pockets and drinking Red Bulls, as usual.

Mike Hawk turns to York Hunt, lifts his Hot Pocket, and says, "Is it wrong to call it a Hot Pocket if it's cold?"

York gestures at me with his chin and says, "You should

befriend this ninja. He seems like a good guy. And he could prove a valuable ally in your quest to vanquish The Principal."

My other demon, Mike, stamps his foot. "Dude," he says, holding his Hot Pocket at York, shaking it for emphasis. "I've got to warm this bad boy *up*."

My demons disappear between flickers of the lights.

"One of the four exotically beautiful Eastern European girls I mentioned earlier is coming over now," says the ninja. "I'm watching her, but I don't need to because I can sense the presence of everyone around me. My father, who's also a ninja, trained me while I was in the womb, my mother's womb of course, she's a terrific lady, I can't say enough great things about her, you should meet her sometime, I think you'd really like her, and, like I was saying, my father trained me to sense the presence of everyone around me."

I reach into my locker, grab my smokes and lighter, stick a fresh cigarette between my lips, and light it. "He trained you in the womb?" I jut out my lower lip and blow smoke in front of my face.

"That's right. Using age-old ninja techniques, he trained me in the use of various fighting styles and weapons while I was still in the womb."

Casually, leaning back against my locker, I look over, and check out the four girls he's been talking about. They're exotically beautiful all right. I don't know how he can tell they're Eastern European, though. "How'd you get weapons in there?"

"My father knew a guy."

"Ah." I watch as one of the four exotically beautiful girls leaves her smiling friends and starts walking toward us. In the horror survival hall, she's a goddess. Her shiny black hair bounces with each of her steps. It floats weightlessly, falls, and dances. She turns and looks back at her three beautiful friends who urge her on, clinging to each other for support, like the suspense is killing them. When the goddess turns back towards us, laughing, a few strands of raven hair twirl in front of her face, but she sweeps the darkness away with one elegant hand, like it's nothing.

"When it was time for my birth," continues the ninja, "I decided I wanted to set out on my own for a while, to be independent: to find myself and see the world. When I say the world, I mean America. The doctor planned to deliver me via C-section, but I'd never allow anyone to cut my mother. It took every ounce of self-restraint I had not to kill all the people who'd even *considered* cutting my mother. When they were gathered for the surgery, I slipped, undetected, from my mother. With the umbilical cord in one hand, I jumped off the table. With my free hand, I grabbed a scalpel off a nearby tray. The umbilical cord pulled tight when I was a few inches from the ground. I cut myself loose. I dropped into the fighting stance. No one noticed. Suddenly the alarms connected to the monitors attached to my mother informed the doctor and nurses that something was amiss. In the confusion, I made my escape. I kept the scalpel in case anyone tried to stop me. No one did. They found me six months later, just outside Raleigh, working construction. When interviewed, my coworkers confessed they were never aware I was a baby."

"Hey," I say, before the goddess can reach us, "allow me to introduce myself." I hold out my hand. "I'm Guy Boy Man, which, I admit, is pretty weird, because I'm neither Asian nor a series of keywords to search for gay porn, or for heterosexual porn, if you're a chick, which you aren't."

"Hi, Guy Boy Man," he says, taking my hand, shaking it. "I'm Sweetie Honey."

CHAPTER THREE:
She Has A Tongue-Piercing But That Doesn't Mean Anything

The exotically beautiful Eastern European girl wearing purple high heels, thigh-high purple-and-black horizontally striped leggings, a black skirt, and a tight purple T-shirt reaches Sweetie Honey. "Hi." She lifts her shoulders and holds them up for a moment to apologize for interrupting. When she sees it's cool, she lowers her shoulders, looks Sweetie up and down, and bites her lower lip, sexily.

Sweetie turns to his locker. He lets his backpack slip off his shoulder and catches the strap in one hand before it hits the ground. "Hi," he says, heroically. There's something so daring and bold about the way he says, "Hi." Seriously. If he said "Hi" to you, you'd probably follow him into combat. Not that he'd need your help or anything.

In her left hand, hanging down by her side, the gorgeous girl holds a laptop and a textbook. Of the four girls, all of whom have bangs and bobs, this girl has the darkest, blackest hair. Her purple T-shirt is tight enough to reveal she isn't wearing a bra and to suggest the shape of her medium-sized breasts. Her short black skirt reveals a few tantalizing inches of her long shapely legs' flesh before they disappear into her horizontally striped black and purple leggings. Now that she's closer, I see her leggings are covered with fishnets that have small diamonds, which are covered with fishnets that have bigger diamonds. The diamonds are empty. She smiles and holds out her hand to Sweetie. "I'm Oana."

"Nice to meet you, Oana." Shaking her hand, Sweetie is so cool you could use him to ship lettuce.

"Listen," says Oana, seriously, when they let go of each other's hands. "You're probably wondering about my exotic beauty."

"Sure."

"Well it's the result of years of genetic research done by a group of diabolical scientists in former Soviet bloc countries."

Sweetie nods. "I figured it was probably something like that." He unzips his backpack.

"Their goal was to breed and then modify, behaviourally, attractive women to infiltrate various governments by marrying or having affairs with high-ranking male officials." Staring at Sweetie's chest, Oana's mouth stays open a little, and her luscious pink tongue plays behind her perfect white teeth.

"So the diabolical scientists were men." Leaving his ninja outfit in the backpack, Sweetie pulls out a textbook and examines it.

"They were men for the most part." Oana frowns. "Did you deduce that from the fact that, traditionally, males have been considered more likely to become scientists and so, subconsciously at least, teachers have encouraged them more than their female counterparts?"

"No. I assumed they were men because they thought you could rise to positions of power more easily through your sexuality than through your intellect." Disgusted, Sweetie slams the textbook into his locker. Metal clangs when it impacts.

"Actually, they didn't. It's just much easier to breed beauty than it is to breed political ambition and cunning." With both arms straight, Oana holds her laptop and textbook in front of her. "Also, sadly, women have a harder time succeeding in governmental life than men do."

Sweetie turns on her. "Are you making excuses for diabolical Eastern European scientists?"

She looks at him, wide-eyed. "No. Of course not."

Her sincerity calms him. "Good." He pulls another textbook from his backpack. "Just checking."

"So what's your name?"

"Sweetie Honey." His right bicep bulges against the side of his manly chest as he studies the back of this book.

"Of course it is." She reaches out and puts her hand on his swelling arm. "It has to be. I can't think of anything else to call you."

"Honey is the family name. My mom named me Sweetie."

Oana caresses Sweetie's arm, mesmerized by it. "Your mom sounds like a saint."

"She is. She has a tongue-piercing but that doesn't mean anything." With his square-jawed chin, Sweetie Honey gestures over at the other three exotically beautiful Eastern European girls watching him from the end of the hall. "Who are your friends?"

Oana doesn't even look. "Iulia, Marta, and Agata." When she notices the way Sweetie Honey is eyeing her, she adds, "In Eastern Europe, we are suspicious of the 'h' and the 'j.' The 'h,' when it is small, looks like a chair. Is it an electric chair? We don't know. Is it a regular chair sitting on a trap door? Again, we don't know. When it's big, the 'H' is always dangerous. If you pass under it, maybe the bar will fall on you. If you go over it, possibly the bar will shoot up when you're halfway across. And the 'j,' whether big or small, is always a hook. In Eastern Europe, we don't get caught."

"I don't get caught, either," says Sweetie Honey. "I'm a ninja."

"That's so exciting," says Oana, gasping.

"Are your friends the product of genetic research and behaviour modification, as well?"

"Yes."

Sweetie nods knowingly, probably because before he merely wondered and thought, but he didn't know, and now he does, or thinks so, or is at least willing to let it go.

Oana traces the tips of her fingernails down Sweetie's arm to his strong hand. She clasps it desperately and pulls it toward her, achingly. "The four of us are new to this school, but we're going to be the most popular girls here in no time."

"I wouldn't be surprised. People are so shallow." Sweetie looks down the horror show hall, probably thinking about the cruelty of it all.

With straight legs, Oana leans down dangerously close to the weapon in the front of Sweetie Honey's pants, and she kisses the back of his hand instead of lifting it and possibly annoying him. When she straightens back up, she says, "We haven't received our orders yet, about whom we should marry, or have affairs with, so we just kind of glom onto any alpha males around."

Sweetie Honey glares at her, critically. "You should resist your genetic imperative."

Suddenly Big Max starts pushing his way through the crowd in the hallway toward us. In warning, the raven on my shoulder bounces, lifting its open beak toward Big Max, cawing. Big Max strides right up to Oana. "What are you doing?" he demands. "I'm the most popular guy in school. If you and your friends want to be the most popular girls in school"—he pokes his thumb into his chest—"you have to be with me."

"Get lost," says Oana, annoyed. "We already know about you. Your popularity is entirely sports-related. While it's true you might become a professional athlete someday and make millions of dollars, you'll never be as amazing as Sweetie Honey." She looks at Sweetie dreamily.

"I'm really upset by this stuff you're saying," says Big Max, frowning. "I'm going to take out my hurt and frustration on this *monkey*." He points at Sweetie Honey.

Everyone gasps.

"Wait a minute," I tell the gathering crowd, holding out my hand at them to stop. "Most of us are strict Creationists. Maybe Big Max isn't. Maybe Big Max acknowledges the objective scientific validity of the theory of evolution, in which case, calling Sweetie Honey a monkey *isn't* derogatory because, according to evolution, we're *all* primates. Is that it, Big Max?"

"No," says Big Max, cracking his knuckles. "It was a racial slur. I'm a strict Creationist too."

I stick my cigarette between my lips, set down my bottle of whiskey, reach back, and pull out one of my nine-millimetres. I point it at Big Max. "Big Max seems troubled! He could be armed! I'm going to take him down!" I pull back the slide to chamber a round, but a round goes flying out when I do, because I'd already chambered a round, but I forgot. "Hold on!" I crouch down, search the school's rubble, pick up the unspent bullet, clean off the debris, pop out the clip, reload the bullet, and slam the clip back home.

N V P F Z

I stand and examine the gun. "Okay I think I'm . . . no." I click off the safety. "Yeah. I'm ready now." I point the nine-millimetre at Big Max again.

In the instant that passes from the time when I put my finger on the trigger but before I can apply pressure to it, Sweetie grabs Big Max's head and slams it into a locker. It happens so fast, it happens exclusively in the past. I don't see or hear anything. I only have vague memories of it. A blur of motion. A sick sound. The lose-your-lunch crunch of bone breaking. The metal crash of instant indentation. One second, Big Max is standing there, larger than life, and living, and the next second he's falling, limp and dead, to the floor.

"That was awesome," I say, staring down at Big Max, lowering my nine-millimetre. Fluidly, the colour red pours from his smashed face. The way it forms a dark pool, growing outwards, is beautiful.

"Sweetie Honey," exclaims Oana, throwing her arms around him, "you're a hero!"

"Heroes never admit they're heroes," says Sweetie, coolly.

"But they're still heroes, right?"

"Even more so."

I click the safety back on, stick my nine-millimetre back into the holster on my lower back, straddle Big Max, squat down over him, and stick a finger into the red oil slick of his blood. I draw lines extending outwards from it, like rays of a crimson star. The hallway lights strobe off every time I go back for more "paint." They turn back on each time I reach the end of a "sun beam." They animate my work. When I lift my finger, after I'm done turning blood into a childish red giant, I look at the mysterious substance on my fingertip. It pales on my skin, like a chameleon. For some reason, I stick my finger, covered in the stuff of life, which is also the stuff of death, into my mouth, and suck it off. It tastes like pennies, little bits of money. I'm not worried about catching anything from it because life is an STD and I've already got it.

Still with one leg on either side of what was recently Big Max and is now just his big dead body, I stand back up, and look down at him. His use of performance-enhancing drugs, his frequent absences from practice, and his selfish play on the field are all that kept him from becoming a zombie, and now he's dead. His blood keeps flowing. When it's almost touching my right shoe, I think about stepping away, but then, for some reason, I don't, and the red fluid pours into the tread valleys on the bottom of my runner.

Suddenly a zombie teacher comes ambling out of a classroom. With his arms outstretched in our direction, he stumbles toward us. He's wearing the same stainless steel muzzle the zombie students wear, but not the helmet. His hands are untied too. He is, however, chained to his classroom. Cuffed to his right ankle, the chain is thick. It's long enough to let him enter the hallway but it prevents him from travelling far. The links clank on the floor as he pushes his way through the kids taking pictures and shooting video with their cell phones. The zombie teacher wears a shredded dark blue sweater through which I can see his mottled grey-white torso. He sports pairs of blood-smeared brown pants and excrement-caked brown loafers that I can smell from here. He has a comb-over, but it isn't combed over. The bald top of his head is exposed. The long hair he grew to cover his baldness now hangs pointlessly. When he reaches us, the zombie teacher moans.

"This teen"—I explain loudly, pointing my gun down at Big Max repeatedly—"may have been troubled. He may not have been," I admit, "but that's beside the point. He made us fear for our lives, which, you know, suck, but they're all we got, so sometimes, when necessary, we have to defend them with lethal force, and sometimes we have to defend them with lethal force even when it isn't necessary, as a lesson to those who might, in the future, make us fear for our lives, which will still, undoubtedly, suck, but will still be all we've got."

The zombie teacher groans.

"What'd he say?" I ask one of the bystanders.

"He thinks the young man is dead."

"No, he's okay."

The zombie teacher groans again.

"Oh come on," says Sweetie, irritated. Effortlessly, he picks up Big Max by the back of the pants and shirt collar. Sweetie tries to balance him so he's standing on his own, but Big Max's legs won't cooperate. "He's fine. See?"

The zombie teacher moans.

Sweetie lets go. Big Max collapses to the floor again. After a second of staring down at him, Sweetie lifts his shoulders and smiles awkwardly at the zombie teacher.

The zombie teacher stumbles away down the hall. When he reaches the end of his chain, he tries to keep going. He can't. He pulls at what holds him back, over and over, mindlessly. I just stare at him, revolted.

Recently I announced that, starting on Monday, zombie teachers and zombie students would *no longer* be allowed at this school. The opportunity to go to a school that isn't infested with zombies probably explains all the new students: the cute pink-haired girl with a unicorn that follows her around, Baby Doll15; the handsome African-American ninja, Sweetie Honey; and the four exotically beautiful Eastern European girls, Oana, Iulia, Marta, and

Agata. Hey. I just thought of something: Why didn't the four exotically beautiful Eastern European girls make a play for me? Admittedly, I'm no ninja. But I *am* alpha. No. If there were something that came *before* alpha, that's what I'd be. I'm *pre*-alpha. That's how alpha I am. (I'm also post-omega, if you're keeping track.) I'm a pirate *and* a spiritual leader! (I know that's redundant, but I like to emphasize both aspects.) Maybe the four exotically beautiful girls heard I'm not interested in a serious relationship. I'm not dating anyone exclusively. I mean, I'm *exclusively* dating attractive girls, but I'm not dating any *one* of them exclusively.

"I'm new to this school," says Sweetie, staring down at what remains of Big Max. "What do you usually do with your dead bodies here?"

"Bury them," I say.

Sweetie nods. "That's what we did at my old school."

"Sweetie," says Oana, ignoring the dead body of Big Max. "My parents"—she makes air quotation marks around the word "parents"—"are gone for the long weekend, so after school, Agata, Marta, Iulia, and I are going back to my place to explore our sexual orientation and erogenous zones. Do you want to come?"

"I guess," says Sweetie, shrugging.

"Great!" exclaims Oana. "See you after school!" She hurries away, cheerfully.

Sweetie starts unpacking his backpack again.

I look into his locker, at all the tools of the ninja. "Hey, Sweetie," I say. "Can I see your sword? The long one?" I point at it.

"I took a vow to never unsheathe it unless I intend to kill someone," says Sweetie, seriously.

I nod, tapping ashes on the hallway floor. With the two fingers between which my cigarette is pinched, I point. "What about that kid over there?" I ask.

CHAPTER FOUR:
I'm Really Wasted Right Now

It's very early in the morning on Friday, a school holiday, and I'm about ten hours late for my date with Baby Doll15. The sun isn't up yet. The sun never rises. The sun never sets, either. It's the Earth spinning that makes it seem like it does, but it doesn't. It's an illusion. A lie. The sidewalks, front lawns, and parked cars. In the neighbourhoods I'm driving through, everything is lit by streetlights and darkness.

I'm really wasted right now. I always drive wasted. You should never drive sober. It's suicidal. When a drunk driver gets in an accident with a sober driver, nine times out of ten (not an actual statistic), the *drunk* driver walks away unscathed, while the *sober* driver, along with his or her entire family, is invariably killed. When you're drunk, and you get in an accident, you go limp, which is, apparently, the best way to go in an accident. Unless it's a sexy accident. My point is this: driving sober is dangerous and not nearly as much fun as driving hammered. When you drive drunk, it always looks like you're coming to a fork in the road. The trick is to keep going straight, between the prongs, because there really is no fork. Sort of like the spoon in *The Matrix*.

I turn on the dash-mounted touch-screen HD satellite TV. Wait. The TV isn't a satellite. It isn't orbiting the vehicle I'm driving. That'd be cool, though. Probably pretty distracting, but cool. No. The satellite TV is called a "satellite TV" because it receives its signal from a man-made satellite orbiting the Earth.

Oh, to be a manmade satellite! In the cold, in the dark! A receiver, a transmitter! Unaffected by everything! Retaining nothing! It hurts so much not to be, and instead, or rather, at the same time, to be!

I look away from the TV and back at the road. I'm drunk-driving for safety, but to double up on safety, I'm driving a bulldozer. It isn't one of those puny little bulldozers you see toppling trees sometimes. No. It's an enormous *mining* bulldozer. It's the kind of bulldozer you'd use to push down a mountain. I find that when I get in an accident while I'm driving a gigantic bulldozer, it doesn't really bother me. And huge bulldozers are also excellent for zombie outbreaks because there are always a bunch of abandoned cars and pickup trucks in your way. The driver's area of my bulldozer is encased in (pock-marked) bullet- and sound-proof glass, overlaid by a chain-link cage that locks in order to protect occupants (me) from the undead and the few living people who escape the Zombie Acceptance Test and fend for themselves in a post-apocalyptic wasteland. Anyway, my bulldozer rumbles, crashes, and grinds happily down the street.

I click through a few channels on TV. I don't actually fail to find anything worth watching. I never fail, okay? That's why The Principal of Scare City High is in so much trouble. I vowed to remove him from power, shortly after I discern his whereabouts, and I never fail. The zombie teachers who suggest I do, occasionally, fail are stupid stinking zombie liars! Yeah. I don't actually fail to find anything worth watching; the TV fails to provide anything worth watching.

Stupid TV!

I love TV. Don't get me wrong.

I turn my attention back to the road. What's this? I seem to have driven my gargantuan bulldozer through a suburban home. I look over my shoulder at the devastation in my wake. Oh well. I twist my head back around and steer the bulldozer onto a new street. I had to make a turn this way later in any event.

As I mentioned earlier, I'm going to pick up Baby Doll15 in the early hours of the morning for our date—I'm ten hours late—and for safety, firstly, I'm drunk; secondly, I'm driving an enormous mining bulldozer; and to *triple* up on safety, I'm wearing a blue bomb-disposal suit, which is sort of like a bullet-proof vest for your whole body and head. I brought one for Baby Doll15 too. People in America have a tendency to shoot at you when you're driving down their street in a huge bulldozer. Or a regular car. Or if you're walking down the sidewalk.

On my way to pick up Baby Doll15, I total over 400 cars. On purpose. I total thirty-five by mistake. I also drive through eight houses. Luckily, when I get to Baby Doll15's place, I don't need to honk the horn because Baby Doll15 comes running out to greet me as soon as I pull up outside, probably because I rattled the hell out of all the windows in her house and knocked a bunch of crappy ceramic things off the shelves. It's also lucky because the bulldozer doesn't have a horn. That I'm aware of.

Gunfire is ringing out from all the neighbouring houses when Baby Doll15 dashes out. With her hands over her ears, she zigzags toward the bulldozer, briefly ducking down and taking cover behind a parked car. Then she races toward me again. Fortunately, I dispatched a large contingent of my absurd number of disposable bodyguards in advance of my arrival for just this sort of occasion. They lay down covering fire, quickly suppressing the neighbourhood malcontents. When the gunfire dies down, I open the bulldozer's cage, climb out, and drag out the extra blue bomb-disposal suit I brought for Baby Doll15. It isn't extra blue. It's regular blue. I guess it's more navy blue than regular blue, and I suppose you could argue it's extra blue if you haven't seen anything blue in years and the sun hits it just right when you're looking at it or whatever. I'm just saying. It's extra in the sense that I don't need it for myself. I brought it for Baby Doll15.

She greets me cheerfully and a little breathlessly. I don't know if she's breathless because of her recent run through heavy crossfire or because of me. It's probably the crossfire but you never know. Baby Doll15's cotton-candy pink hair is centre-parted and thick; it's straight until it reaches the tops of her ears: there it flows down in voluminous waves that stretch out to the width of her shoulders. Her eye makeup is smoky black. She's wearing a baby-pink baby doll over thigh-high white leggings and pink stilettos. Her lips are candy-apple red. She gives me a friendly kiss on the cheek of my bomb-disposal helmet. "How did your strategy session go?" she asks, remembering our earlier conversation.

"It was great," I say. "I even ran drills. Not exercises. Actual drills. In case I have to vigorously interrogate someone."

"Cool," she says, smiling.

"Sorry I'm late."

"It's okay."

Her white unicorn comes strutting out of the house. Startled, one of my bodyguards shoots at it.

"Hold your fire," I yell, dropping Baby Doll15's bomb-disposal suit. I lift my arms as best I can with the limited mobility of the suit. I try to hold up my hands like, stop.

The unicorn charges the bodyguard who dared shoot at it, goring him through the forehead. The unicorn lifts the dead bodyguard and turns around slowly, in a brutal warning to all my other bodyguards. When it's confident they've all seen, the unicorn lowers its head and lets the dead bodyguard flop onto the ground. Then it walks over to us.

"Hey, unicorn," I say, pleasantly.

It looks at me, snorts, and looks away.

"Okay, fine. Be like that. I don't care. I've got plenty of friends. Real friends. Not mythical ones."

"Come on, you guys," says Baby Doll15, trying to make the peace.

I cross my arms, turn away, and shake my head, hurt.

"So are we going straight to your castle or what, Guy Boy Man?"

Gothic castles are impossible to find in America, but, during a series of exciting adventures I can't be bothered to relate here, I managed to acquire one, with a little help from an *un*real-estate agent.

"I suppose," I say, still turned away, with my arms still crossed.

"Come on, Guy Boy Man," says Baby Doll15, moving in front of me so I can see her. "Don't let the unicorn get to you. Please? I need your help, remember?"

"Yeah, you're right," I say, uncrossing my arms. "I'm sorry. I'm just a really sensitive person."

"It's okay," she smiles.

"I'm sorry I called you mythical," I tell the unicorn. "You just haven't been seen since Biblical times." I turn to Baby Doll15. "I brought you an extra blue bomb-disposal suit." I bend over, pick it up, and hold it out to her. "Well, it's not extra blue."

"I love it!" She tries to take it from me, but it's so heavy it falls to the ground, and it pulls her most of the way forward.

After I help her get into it, and up and into the bulldozer, she asks me, through her bomb disposal helmet, "What about the unicorn?"

"I was going to get some of my bodyguards to help me strap it to the roof. Is that cool?"

"I guess so."

I close the door, climb down the bulldozer, walk in front of it, and look around, but the unicorn has disappeared, at least seemingly, not that there's any difference. I do a complete three-sixty. No unicorn. I even look up. Can unicorns fly? I don't know. I put my hands on my hips, staring at the spot where I last saw the unicorn. Powers of invisibility, maybe? Carefully, I walk forward, waving my hands around in front of me, trying to find the unicorn by feel. I keep my head turned to the side. If that stupid unicorn pokes out my eye with its spiralled horn, I'm going to kill it with a hatchet! A thorough hand-search of the unicorn's last known location yields no positive results. I climb back up the bulldozer and knock on the cage. Baby Doll15 turns so she can see me.

I'm frowning and biting my lower lip. "Are you really attached to that unicorn?"

"I kind of love it," she admits.

"I may have lost it."

"May have?" she says, eyeing me.

"Might have?"

"I'm not questioning your grammar."

"Okay, well, yeah. There are certain things I don't know

about unicorns. Like, for example, can they fly? Or can they jump so high and far it really makes no difference? Not that they jump so high it doesn't make a difference, because, obviously, if they jump really high and far it's going to make a difference, at least in comparison with their initial position, although, as you may or might already know, from having seen and heard my sermons on HowToEndHumanSuffering. com, I believe all distance, time, and perception thereof is a trick of the mind, and there is really only one thing, one moment, and one place, and there's no separating them, and everything else is an illusion, the illusion of difference, and anyway, what I'm basically trying to say is, I don't know what the hell is going on with your unicorn right now."

"Unicorns can look after themselves," she says, turning away and staring straight ahead. "Let's just go."

"Is that a general rule? I mean. Do you have to feed them? Do you have to put out a bowl of water for them and take them for regular walks and, you know, that kind of thing? Or do they just look after themselves?"

"Please, let's just go, Guy Boy Man."

"I was only trying to express interest in something I thought was close to your heart," I say, sighing, climbing into the bulldozer. "Bitch."

When we get to my gothic castle, the unicorn is there, waiting for us. There are a couple of dead bodyguards lying around who, apparently, didn't receive my "hold your fire" order in regard to the unicorn, which I made sure was relayed ahead of us from Baby Doll15's house, and there are a bunch of Mexicans running to the scene with body-bags and garden hoses. The unicorn stares at me as I park the bulldozer. Maybe it wants something from me. Feed? Some sort of magic oats? I'm telling you right now if that unicorn wants magic oats from me, it's going to be disappointed because I don't have any magic oats!

Right when I'm about to turn off the bulldozer, I glance at the dash-mounted touch-screen HD satellite TV. Before I can turn it off, I see one of those commercials advertising (black) kids starving to death and dying of easily prevented diseases like malaria. What are they *selling*? I can't figure it out. Nobody is ever going to help those (black) kids, so why do they keep trying to make us feel bad about it? Forget it. I'm not going to feel bad. They're not my (black) kids. You know what they say a mosquito net costs? Ten dollars. Is it a *designer* mosquito net? Is it a *gold* mosquito net? Ten dollars is *way* too much. If the mosquito net cost a dollar, that'd be different. (Nine dollars.) For the price of *one* of their mosquito nets, you could get *ten* of my reasonably priced mosquito nets. (I'm not actually offering one-dollar mosquito nets. I'm just saying.)

The huge doors of my castle are opened and Baby Doll15 and I sweep inside. The enormous scope of the structure is easier to see from within. The open space is oppressive. The ceilings are so vaulted and the rooms are so massive, you feel insignificant. It doesn't matter where you turn, or how often. It's always dizzying. Whether you look up, stumble to a wall, or fall to the ground, all you find is stone. The brightly lit priceless works of art hanging by their necks everywhere are no cause for celebration. The stained-glass windows depicting religious scenes are always dark in the night.

"Who are they?" gasps Baby Doll15, noticing a group of beautiful girls gathered in a room just off the main entrance. "They're *gorgeous*."

It's first thing in the morning and, gathered in a room just off the main entrance, a group of beautiful girls shines in chandelier and candlelight, drinking red wine from big crystal goblets.

N V P F Z

"Some of my hot young female followers," I answer, guiding Baby Doll15 by the arm.

"Why are they dressed like schoolgirls?"

"Because they're schoolgirls."

"We don't wear uniforms at our school."

"They go to a school where they do," I sigh. "Don't make things so complicated, Baby Doll15."

"I didn't know I was."

"None of us ever did."

"I'm not sure I . . ." She's quick-walking in her high heels, trying to keep up with me. "Never mind."

I (inadvertently) paid attention to one of those starving kid commercials the other day. (I couldn't find the remote, nor could I reach the screen to touch it. Are we *ever* going to get thought-screen TV?) The (white) announcer said 28,000 (black) kids starve to death every day. Every day! That's criminal! What kind of monsters (zombies) are having kids in barren wastelands devoid of the barest necessities, namely drinking water, readily available nutritious food, proper waste disposal, shelter, electricity, education, clothing, and (lots and lots of) birth control? It's an outrage. The monsters (zombies) must be stopped!

But it seems to me, at the rate the (black) kids are starving to death, (thankfully) they'll all be dead soon. They'll *certainly* be dead before competition among (not really) equals acting in a (not really) mutually beneficial manner can bring down the price of mosquito nets from ten dollars to one, the price at which (I still won't donate, but I'll at least think) it is reasonable. Unfortunately, some of the starving (black) kids will (stubbornly) cling to life, so I set my (staggering) intellect to the problem that has stumped (none of) the greatest minds of my generation. (The greatest minds of my generation are playing MMORPGs.)

I lead Baby Doll15 up one of the three steep stone

staircases ascending from the foyer. At the top, I pull her down a brightly lit stone corridor. Her stilettos click. The clicks echo.

Initially, I'd hoped to solve the problem of starving (black) children by killing them all, along with their zombie parents, but my team of high-powered attorneys advised me against it. They said that's "genocide." "Genocide is wrong," they said, "not because you're killing a whole bunch of people, but because you're discriminating against the people you're killing." They reminded me of Hitler. (They didn't look like Hitler or anything; they didn't have the moustache; they just said, "Remember Hitler?") "Hitler is so reviled," they explained, "because he killed Jews almost exclusively, and he did it with dispassionate efficiency. Stalin killed far more people, but he didn't discriminate against ethnic or religious groups, and he wasn't very well-organized, so what he did was okay." Because the starving (black) children are almost exclusively African-African (black), my lawyers encouraged me *not* to kill them all because I'd (probably) be reviled. I said I didn't have a problem with that. They said killing them would be expensive. I had a problem with *that*. I like being rich. I plan to stay that way.

In my castle, up the stairs, down the hall, I throw open the doors on a huge stone bedroom. The bed is gigantic and covered with furs and skins. It's surrounded by dozens of thick white candles standing on twisted, curved, and bent wrought-gold stands. The candles have been lit even though there's an inferno raging in the fireplace that's big enough for you to walk in if you crouch down a little, and if you've got nothing against being burned horribly. A big crystal chandelier hangs, lighted, between the fireplace and the bed and its candles. (The crystal chandelier isn't in the way or anything. It hangs over our heads.) The grey stone walls glow golden yellow-white but cold.

"It's really bright in here," says Baby Doll15, concerned.

"I like to see what I'm doing." I take off my pirated Pope pirate hat and spin it away. I reach to the back of my neck, undo my ceremonial robe, and I let it slip to the floor. Now I'm down to my guns and my pirate outfit: breeches and loose-fitting white linen shirt. Eyeing Baby Doll15 and dancing sexily, I start taking off the guns and dropping them seductively on the floor.

After I dropped the idea of genocide, I hoped to solve the problem of the starving (black) children by waiting until climate change raised the sea level, flooding low-lying regions around the world, displacing (and ultimately killing through malnutrition and clashes over aid) millions of (poor light brown) people (who refuse to move inland because they like being close to the beach). Then the (scant) resources directed to those (poor light brown) people could be *re-routed* to help the (starving black) children of the monsters (zombies). I had to dismiss this (great) idea because climate change is moving at a frustratingly slow pace (for my purposes). Besides, the (scant) resources directed to help those (poor light brown) people amounts to little more than can be pirated by the first bureaucrat responsible for distributing them. (*That* pirate isn't letting his or her kids starve to death! No, sir or ma'am!) On a related side note, happily, it's already too late to stop climate change, but the scientists I'm employing to find ways to speed it up have come up with nothing better than to continue polluting, or to pollute more, they said, if that's at all possible. Of course it's possible to pollute more! I'm currently investing heavily in coal-powered plants in Second and Third World countries! I'm also investing heavily in clean American alternatives, and American defence companies, for when we Americans, inevitably, declare war on those who're trying to pollute as much as we do or as much as we used to. I've also got some giant hair driers pointed at what remains of the ice shelf, but that's mostly for show.

"What are you doing?" asks Baby Doll15, horrified.

"Don't worry." I'm doing a striptease and dropping handguns. "The safeties are on."

"Look. I'm kind of nervous about all this. I don't know if I can just, you know, get to it."

"I'm so sorry. Where are my manners? You want to get wasted first." I look around for a bell to ring, or a button to push, something, anything I can use to get someone's attention so Baby Doll15 can get booze. I consider clapping my hands twice or snapping my fingers, but only jerks clap their hands twice or snap their fingers when they're rich and they want something, and even though I'm a jerk and proud of it, I don't always act like a jerk, because sometimes you've got to keep the jerkhood in check; otherwise, the truly inspired moments of jerkery go unnoticed, blending in with all-too-many lesser acts of jerkism. "Hey!" I finally yell. "Can we get some alcohol in here or what?"

"I don't want anything to drink," says Baby Doll15, with her arms crossed in front of her and with her hands covering her shoulders, uncomfortable.

"Cancel the booze!" I yell. More quietly I say, "Then what do you want?"

"I don't know. Maybe you could give me a tour?"

"Of my man-junk?" I ask, confused.

"Your abandoned factory," she says. "I mean, your castle."

I'm still confused. "You want me to refer to my man-junk as 'my castle'?"

"No. I want you to give me a tour of your gothic castle."

"Oh. Yeah. Sure." I walk to the doors and kick them as hard as I can. Remembering they don't open that way, I pull them and leave the bedroom, heading for the stairs. "Come on."

Baby Doll15 hurries after me. Her high heels slow her down.

I was slowed by the problems with genocide and climate change, but I'm pleased to say I discovered a way to stop those terrible commercials featuring upsetting images of, and stories about, (black) kids. The solution was inherent to the problem. The commercials advertising (black) kids starving to death, and dying of easily prevented diseases like malaria, weren't selling anything! That's bad business! Why waste money advertising despair? It's one of the few things (white) people don't want to (intentionally) buy (consciously). But I understood the advertisers' dilemma. What resources can you plunder from a barren wasteland filled with zombies and starving (black) kids and (black) kids dying of malaria? That's when it hit me. (Black) kids! To solve the problem of (black) kids starving to death and dying of malaria, someone (not me personally) should sell (black) kids!

When I'm quite a ways out, down the hall, and I've left Baby Doll15 far behind, I stop abruptly and quit trying to hide my irritation. "Are you actually *toddling* right now?" I turn on her angrily. "Do you need a stroller? Do you want me to get you a stroller? Do you want me to push you around in a stroller?"

"I'm sorry," she squeaks. "These shoes don't fit well, but they're so pretty. I stuffed them with paper." She stops, crosses one leg in front of the other, and leans down. "I'll just take them off."

"Don't," I say. "I hate feet." I start heading back to the

stairs again. "This is all bedrooms," I call back to her, jerking my thumb over my shoulder. Still walking, I mutter, "I should have some stupid person make a stupid tour movie of this stupid place so I don't have to give stupid tours every stupid minute." When I get back to the staircase, I wait for her, with my arms crossed, tapping my foot, like a gentleman. "Come on, come on," I call. When she catches up, I take her arm to make sure she doesn't trip, slip, or fall down the steep stone stairs. At the bottom, I let go of her and make a left. It's a right from the main entrance. The reason there's no good set of directions for anything is because it all depends on where you start, and how.

How we (not me personally) go about selling the (black) kids is crucial. Obviously, we shouldn't sell *all* the (black) kids. We should leave behind *some* (black) kids, so we (not me personally) can help them. I'm really optimistic about this plan. There's a huge (white) market for (black) kids! Okay, yeah. I know what you're thinking. The (black) kids have bloated bellies and discoloured hair. Who's going to want them? Well, I'm confident if you give the (black) kids some menial jobs, wait until they get their first paycheques, and sell them a couple of Cokes and a few bags of chips, they'll be as good as new. Scarred, obviously, by their lives of (unspeakable) suffering, but other than that. . . . And I'm confident thousands and thousands of (white) women would love to adopt a child. Probably not a black one, which is wrong of them, racist, but it doesn't matter, because beggars can't be choosers. There's also a second (sketchier) market that we (not me personally) could explore if the "adoption" idea doesn't pay sufficient dividends.

On the main floor of my castle, I make my way through rooms empty with art. Next to me, Baby Doll15 gasps. She's keeping pace with me now. Each of the spacious rooms through which we're walking would've honoured any museum, but the priceless works of art in my castle aren't hidden behind bullet-proof glass. They aren't hooked up to alarms. If they're paintings, sketches, or illuminated manuscripts, they sit on easels. If they're smaller sculptures, they sit on stands. If they're bigger works, they stand on their own. Baby Doll15 and I weave our way around them. Most of my statues are outside.

Everything has been damaged here. In the art wing of my castle. A bust has been pushed to the floor and left there. Is the empty stand art now, or is the broken bust? Is any of it art now? Is none of it? Is nothing? A Da Vinci sketch has been hacked up with a knife. Do the angles of the slices have meaning? Does their position relative to what remains of the sketch? Nothing has been taken away. I like the look of ruined things. I find destroyed things, things beyond salvation, the most beautiful of all. Like the world. My followers and I ritually engage in orgies of destruction. Paintings, sculptures, signed first editions. We light them on fire. Have you ever seen a Van Gogh burning? There's nothing like it. That thick paint melting and dripping. The colours on the floor. What do they represent? Have you ever kicked your leg through a Monet? Punched your fist through a Picasso? Have you ever urinated on a first-edition Hemingway? What a (communist) waste to hang (and kill) these pieces and shelve (forget) these books in (torture chambers called) museums and (graveyards called) libraries where anyone and everyone can see them. For next to nothing. All that work. To distract zombies from their zombie lives. To give them the illusion of escape where there is none, where there can be none. The artist is the enemy. He and she must be destroyed. They are living servants of the undead. They make zombie non-life worth un-living. Zombies *deserve* to be imprisoned in the prisons they've created. They should be *disallowed* colours, textures, or words in their cells. They should go insane with their insanity.

Baby Doll15 doesn't ask questions about what's been destroyed. She takes in everything silently. Either she doesn't need to know why, she already knows why, or she's scared to find out. Regardless, she doesn't criticize my "lack of respect." She doesn't sound off on my "wastefulness." She doesn't condemn me for depreciating the priceless.

A wise man once said, "It's fun to do bad things."

Value is subjective, and through a series of exciting adventures I can't be bothered to relate here, I became free in the sense that I realized past the point of belief, past the point of knowledge, past the point of being, that I'm neither an object nor a subject, so I can't objectify anything—art, the world, myself—or subject anything—everything, nothing, what I am, what is within me and without me, in all its various forms and guises—to the faulty judgement of any mind disconnected from the whole, which both is and isn't, resembling something like the number zero, which exists, in a sense, but represents something that doesn't, or a black hole (African-American hole), from which all springs, returns, and never leaves to begin with or end.

I can only destroy. Add to the madness.

"Where are we going?" asks Baby Doll15, finally.

"That's an excellent question."

Will this path lead me from despair?

Have you ever heaved an ancient piece of Chinese pottery out the window and watched it shatter into the past from which it never came? (It was always made now.) Have you ever seen the pieces? (It was never whole.) Sometimes the mess is for the best. (It was never meant to be. It was actually meant *not* to be.) It's too late. Sometimes you need to see for yourself that it's impossible to put it back the way it was. (It never was the way it was.) Trying is a waste of time. (Time is waste; therefore, trying is a waste of waste.) We all sit idly by while entropy traipses through our disorderly worlds, in shrinking spirals of accelerating chaos. Futurists are historians.

"Do you want to tour the grounds too?" I ask Baby Doll15, still walking through the museum part of my castle.

"I don't think so," calls Baby Doll15, falling behind.

"Then I'll just tell you about it. My castle is lighted in the night, but when we pulled up, maybe you didn't see its tall thin spires straining to pierce the sky, to let in the black, or to let out the blue. It also has gargoyles. Gargoyles are awesome."

"I like gargoyles too," agrees Baby Doll15. She has to almost yell it. Her high heels aren't clicking behind me anymore. They're making more distant sounds, like ticks of the second (or third) hand on an analog wristwatch when it's away from your ears, hanging by its throat at your side.

I stop and wait for her, crossing my arms and shaking my head, patiently. If I were impatient, I'd shoot her. Then she'd hurry up. "I think of my gargoyles as protectors. They guard my castle and serve as warnings to suckers, fools, and little bitches. They're like my raven. My raven is probably out with my gargoyles right now. Watching over us. I've also got a bunch of tortured-looking religious statues all over the grounds. They're pretty cool. The girls really like them. It's the idea of eternal love, I guess."

"Do you?" asks Baby Doll15, finally catching up. She puts her hands on her knees, trying to catch her breath. "Do you believe in eternal love?"

"No."

"Well, I do," she says, tired but defiant.

"Good for you. And no, I don't want to hear your poems." I start walking again.

She starts following again. "What are you talking about? I don't have any poems."

"Of course you do."

She doesn't say anything for a while. Then she says, "I wouldn't read them to you anyway."

The next room in my castle is a fully stocked two-story library. "Books," I say, waving my hand around, un- and disinterested. The library has rolling ladders you can move from side to side to get to the ones on the second floor. I hardly ever read, but sometimes I come here to my library, move the ladders around, and climb them. I like the ladders. They're fun.

The trouble with the books in my library is they're not real. They're real in the sense that they're books. They have pages marked with letters and words (i.e., symbols) arranged in a sort of order. After one learns how to read the symbols, and does so, thereby deciphering them, perhaps not as the author intended but, for better or worse (if there are such things, and there aren't), associating the symbols with their various meanings (i.e., definitions), choosing the meaning (or meanings) that seem most appropriate when taken in context, these symbols become the reader and the reader becomes the symbols (inasmuch as one informs the other), creating an impression. These books (symbols, black markings, or the white space that *fails* to be blotted out, or the white space that *succeeds* in avoiding oblivion) that are readers that are authors, creating their own impressions through reading (or, rather, writing) the text with the meanings (definitions) to which they have access and which seem most appropriate given the context (the context is changeable too) sometimes create thoughts (or seem to). Others, feelings. A few, both. But they're not real. Again, they're not fake books. They're not empty boxes or covers separated by blank pages. They're regular books. But they're not what they contain and what they contain is not a book. We've been so misled. Books close your eyes and manipulate you. There's nothing wrong with that until, invariably, the zombies start walking toward you. Sometimes you open your eyes and see the zombies in time. Most of the time, you don't.

I leave the library. "This is a drawing room, where I draw." I move into another room, bringing all my baggage. "This is a sitting room, where I sit." I walk out into an area where another group of my hot young female followers is gathered, watching the morning's entertainment. (The party never stops in my castle.) The girls are all dressed anachronistically. In their loose but sexy dresses, in their stockings, with their hair pasted to their heads, twisted in curls on their foreheads, this group of my followers is dressed like flappers: frivolous young women from the 1920s. They're slinking in huge antique chairs. In a couple of cases, they're sitting sideways on each other's laps and lightly trailing their fingertips over each other's bare arms. They're drinking red wine from big crystal goblets, talking amongst themselves, smiling, laughing, and sometimes pointing at the show.

Tattooed and pierced "pin-up girls" are taking turns situating themselves in classic pin-up-girl poses, adding to the sense of timelessness (or the meaninglessness of time) created (or highlighted) by my followers. The pin-up girls—with their early- to mid-twentieth century hairdos and their bright red lipstick, in their garter belts, hosiery, and high heels—try to outdo each other. I stop for a moment, putting my hand on one of my followers' bare shoulders. Immediately, she puts her hand on mine and looks up at me but I keep watching the pin-up girls. I'm not really a tattoo and piercing guy, but there's something about the mix of old (pin-up) and new but not really new (tattoos and piercings on and in pin-up girls) that appeals to me. Then I get bored.

I lead Baby Doll15 away from the party. I whisk her into the south-facing wing of the castle. "Oh my God," she whispers.

Each of these huge rooms has gigantic stained glass windows—some of which stretch from threshold to peak, from the width of the walls to the depths of our collective inexperience—and the windows are blushing with and embarrassed by the early morning sun in the east, filtered through the gloom of grey clouds covering everything. Baby Doll15 and I are bathed in soft light, in water colours: oranges, reds, greens, blues, and yellows. The religious scenes depicted are especially sinister and threatening in their dishonest innocence and immutability.

Obviously, I'm not one of those spiritual leaders who pretends to be a really great guy (not that a woman couldn't be a spiritual leader), and then you find out he or she is really pretty bad. I admit it upfront. I'm terrible. Really. I'm pretty awful. But when I'm here, in the south-facing wing of my castle, in all these rooms I'm leading Baby Doll15 through, with all these (artful) stained glass windows depicting religious scenes, I know I'm not nearly as dreadful as I need to be.

I'm working on it, though.

Back in my bedroom, Baby Doll15 sits on the edge of my bed. My demons, Mike Hawk and York Hunt, are there. As usual, they're eating Hot Pockets and drinking Red Bulls.

N V P F Z

"So are you going to do her or what?" asks Mike Hawk, lifting his Hot Pocket to his mouth and taking a big bite.

"Why are you guys being like this?" I ask, confused. "Usually you advise me against this sort of thing. 'She's evil, don't do it, you're going to regret it,' " I mock. "What's going on?"

"Nothing," says York Hunt, exchanging anxious glances with Mike Hawk. Both of them have mouthfuls of Hot Pocket. Both of them have stopped chewing.

"Something is definitely going on," I insist.

"No, it isn't," chokes Mike Hawk. He's trying, and failing, to be casual.

York Hunt swallows a big lump, nervously. "We're going downstairs." Anxiously, he jerks his head toward the door for Mike Hawk to follow. "You kids get to know each other and do what comes natural."

"You're terrible demons," I mutter, as they leave.

"That's very nice of you to say."

"It's a real pleasure tormenting you, Guy Boy Man," adds Mike Hawk, smiling, with his head stuck in. Then he closes the door.

I slam the door behind them. I take a couple of deep breaths, trying to calm myself. Then I turn to Baby Doll15. She quickly looks down at her hands; they're fidgeting on her lap. She's sitting on the edge of the bed. It's a scary edge, a cliff. Her knees are together, tightly. Her feet don't reach the floor. Her white stocking feet and pink high heels dangle. I walk over to her. I sit beside her.

I lift her chin with my crooked forefinger. I move my lips close to hers, so close to hers, and I stop there. Our eyes are open. We're both looking down, at the nearness. Our eyelashes are whipping at each other and almost touching. I want to kiss this girl and I don't know why. I want to kiss this girl more than any other girl I've ever wanted to kiss. (What's going on? She's only mildly attractive!) I want to kiss her but I don't want to kiss her because then I'll be kissing her. It won't be as wonderful and horrible as this. Unrealized desire. The problem and its apparent solution. It'd be worse to leave it here, or so it seems, so we kiss, once, innocently, gently, and then we part, but before we do, we seem stuck together for a second, glued, and then it gives way.

Her mouth is open and close to mine. I feel her hot breath. I smell its strange sweetness. Her eyes open slowly. They widen, searching both of mine, back and forth, like there's a flower conversation going on between my irises and she doesn't want to miss a petal, or a word. When her lips move toward mine, seemingly almost against her will, like I'm drawing them there, I move my head back slightly to prolong it, this, the moment we're both here, on the edge, before we both fall over, become weightless, and feel the wind trying to catch us, to save us, before we land and die this death we both want, the death of the unknown, where we'll be born again, touching, tasting, feeling, hearing, and seeing everything. I say, "I wonder why my demons want me to be with you."

She grabs my head and forces her lips against mine, shutting me up. Our mouths open and close against each other, saying wordless words, pronouncing nothing except some slow and sweet sound, declaring only willingness, no, eagerness now, and our tongues join in and reach for something they'll never find, and we encode and decipher a new language, communicating, and it's impossible to say if our tongues are working together when they never seem to agree and always seem to be at cross purposes, but they don't seem to ever want to stop.

On the bed, we pull off each other's clothes. We pull off our own clothes if we're having a problem or it's going too slowly. (I tell her to leave on her heels and stockings. And her pearl necklace and golden chain and cross.) There's a momentum to this now. We've been caught in its gravity and it's pulling us toward the centre we'll both soon share. We're breathing hard and both our bodies are feverish and once we're naked and there are no secrets anymore, no secrets that matter anyway, and our hands have dissatisfied themselves, journeying to the places they always wanted to go, only to find they're tourists, we realize we need a place to stay.

I kick down her door.

"This is the position Christians used to convert the heathens," I announce. "I'm in the Christian position. You're in the heathen."

"Oh my God!" she moans. "This is so disappointing!"

Her body is killer. Guns shooting. Hatchets swinging. I'm really looking at it. Especially her boobs. They're big. You should see them.

"Oh yeah, I'm really giving it to you now," I admit.

"I can barely feel a thing!" she cries.

The look on her face keeps changing: one moment she's shocked: wide-eyed and open-mouthed; the next she's in pain she seems to like: her face is scrunched but her jaw works over soundless words.

"I hope this doesn't last much longer!" shouts Baby Doll15.

"It won't," I assure her, glancing down. What's happening below us is disgusting and tragic, beautiful and important, or both.

I know it sounds crass, but I made a study of the vagina. Admittedly, at the time, it was a little awkward for the owners/operators of the vaginas of which I made a study, but they went along with it. I looked at vaginas in soft light, in fluorescence, in harsh white incandescence. I drew diagrams, scribbled notes, entered (male) numbers into (female) formulas and came up with (dissatisfactory) answers. I wasn't happy with the results. I went over my findings time and time again. I kept looking for an error that would nullify my conclusions. But ultimately I failed to find fault with myself. My method was sound. [I'm not saying I used sound, exclusively, to study the vagina. Obviously, I bounced sound waves of different frequency off the vaginas, and I used sonar to fathom their depths, but "sound" was *not* my only tool. (High five.)] Eventually, I had to admit it.

No matter how much I'm drawn to vaginas, they're ugly.

Baby Doll15 frowns. "Is it still in?"

"Yeah."

"Wow," she groans. "This is not what I was hoping for at all."

"I'm really turned on by dissatisfaction."

"You must be so turned on right now!" she cries.

"Yes."

I don't know what floods my mind to convince me otherwise during the prelude to sex, but vaginas are a freak show. (Have you ever noticed how aliens and monsters in sci-fi and horror movies are often vagina-like?) By no means did my study suggest that penises are in any way "better" or "more attractive" than vaginas. I didn't study penises. Penises are not my area of interest. But I suspect a thorough scientific examination of penises would yield similar results (i.e., they're gross too).

"I should have said more than 'yes' back then," I admit,

"but I couldn't think of anything."

"Your penis is so small!" she shouts.

"I know. I used to be really depressed about it but then I realized I didn't care. It's good enough for me. If you're unhappy, that's your problem."

"Then I'm having all kinds of problems right now," she moans. "Oh God! I'm *so* unhappy!"

The vagina appears to have been blown out from within, as if by some great force, possibly an explosion, and all the disgusting bits and bobs on the surface resemble some sort of horrific fallout. I wonder: was I looking at it from the right side?

"Shouldn't it be harder?" whimpers Baby Doll15.

"No, it's always about this difficult."

"I mean your penis."

"Oh. I had sex five times before you came over so I could last longer."

"You shouldn't have!" she says.

I bury my face in the pillow next to her head, in a pile of her hair. It smells like baby shampoo. She breathes hotly in my ear. "Please make things better." The sensation of her lips on my ear is so visceral, it's visual. I can actually see her lips through the sound of their feeling.

"I'm really frustrating the hell out of you, aren't I?" I sneer, lifting my head.

"So much!" she cries. "It's torture but not the good kind!"

"This is awesome."

Something is happening. I don't know how, what, or why. Something is definitely happening. It's happening to me. Maybe it's because she isn't beautiful. Maybe it's because she's just cute. She has room for improvement. In my eyes. I don't know, I don't know, I don't know. It's never been like this for me. It's never meant anything. It's always been about escaping. The moment, the place, myself. Now it's about her, giving something to her, something she doesn't believe in. Angrily, spitefully. I don't believe in it either: The sacredness of this disgusting animal thing. But I want to disillusion her of her disillusions, even though I share them, because I want more for her.

Wait, wait, wait. *What*? I want more for *her*? *Why*? That's crazy. I want more for myself. But maybe by wanting more for *her* I'll get more for myself. Who are you? What are you doing in my head? Are you the zombies? Are you hacking into my brain?

"I wish everything was different!" yells Baby Doll15.

"I'm fantasizing about other girls."

"I wish they were here instead of me too!"

"It'll be over soon."

"That's what you said when we started!"

I look down at her, beneath me. She's so much more than cute now. She seems more beautiful than any girl could possibly be and I know that whether or not I saw her more accurately before, I'll never be able to see her that way again. It'll always be like this, with wonder in her scary eyes and a whimper on her lips. Maybe the zombies are using this girl because she possesses some special pheromone that reduces my immunity to their zombie signal. Is that why my demons urged me to be with her?

Suddenly I want Baby Doll15 to devour my body. (That's worrisome. Could I allow myself to become zombie food?) I want her to drink my blood. (That's less worrisome—vampire make-believe.) I don't want to be inside her just this (admittedly) little bit. I want to *become* her. I want to *be* her, looking at me like she's looking at me, and meaning it. I want to eat *her* body (worrisome; could I become a zombie willingly?). I want to drink *her* blood (less worrisome—vampire make-believe again). I want her to know how I feel.

As the pace increases, I can't look at her anymore. She becomes too gorgeous. I cover her face with one hand and turn her head to the side. She pushes her face against my hand and groans. As I fall faster and faster, and the sound of my body hitting the ground grows in intensity and frequency, she twists out from under my hand and locks me in her eyes. I feel everything bad leave me. For a frantic second I want it back, I don't want it to change her, but then, somehow, I know it won't (i.e., I'm using a condom).

We look at each other, out of breath and sweating, and we don't say anything but we both know exactly what we mean.

CHAPTER FIVE:
There's A Table On A Hill In The Cemetery

Baby Doll15 and I sleep through the day and wake in the night. It's the same night. It's the darkness on this side of twelve instead of the darkness on the (so-called) other side of twelve. The magic prison guards of the calendar haven't attempted and failed to divide it yet. At the witching hour, they'll cast their spells and tell us something has changed when it hasn't. We're always on this side of twelve. The wrong side.

The full moon is a big pearl hanging around the neck of night. The chain is stars. The sky is black and glossy, like the coats of nightmares, wrapping around us. A select group of my hot young female followers and I are in a cemetery foggy with ghosts of the living: it's a heavy fog, lying in the lower parts of the (I should've mentioned this earlier) hilly cemetery; that's how I can still see the sky.

There's a table on a hill in the cemetery. Above the table, a giant leafless oak tree stands. In the tree, my raven stands guard. The table is covered with the periodic table of the elements. The tree's branches stretch over half the table. The branches aren't actually stretched *on* the table. They're above it. In the air. I was going to say the tree's branches stretch over the table in the sky, but the table isn't in the sky, and I don't think the branches are, either. I don't know about you, but I think of the sky as something higher than tree branches. I think of the sky as something black and blue, grey and cloudy. I suppose you could say the sky is all around us and we live in it and I wouldn't argue with you, because if you say we live in the sky, you're crazy, and I try not to argue with crazy people. They're usually right. Anyway, let's recap. Night, fog, moon, cemetery, hill, tree, raven (those are your natural elements), table, hot young female followers, me (those are your unnatural elements.)

Candle flames illuminate the table, the periodic table of the elements, and the faces of my hot young female followers seated around it.

Nearby, the oak's trunk is so thick the girls can't get their arms around it. It took six girls holding hands to hug it properly. Giant leaves cover the ground around the tree, like tears shed over the loss of tears. The leaves lost their creator and their vibrant colours. But the tree lost the most. Its yellowish flowers are gone. Its foliage is torturously nearby but forever gone. The brilliant red protestations before the fall were ignored. Now only soft brown reminders cover the cold green spikes of longish lawn. Soon the snow will come and all of this will be covered with one big lie we'll tell ourselves is white.

A few of the girls wanted to glue fallen leaves back onto the tree but even the lower branches are too high, we don't have any glue, and even if we attached all the dead leaves to the places from which they fell, it wouldn't be the same. It'd be a mockery.

That's why I agree we'll come back later with a ladder and lots of glue. Maybe enough glue to do the whole world.

One of my hot young female followers emerges from

the fog, climbing the hill toward us, carrying the heavy front of her full-length gown. "Baby Doll15 is right behind me," she says, breathless, kissing me on the cheek. "She looks amazing."

All my hot young female followers are dressed similarly and, in this respect, Baby Doll15 is no different. Baby Doll15's high heels click on the stone path that winds up the hill between the grey headstones. She's wearing a corseted gown. Its voluminous skirt is full-length. She holds up the front of it to keep it from dragging on the ground. She doesn't walk as much as glide, and she doesn't glide as much as seduce. One foot crosses in front of the other with every step, moving her hips from side to side, emphasizing them. The corset exaggerates her already exaggerated breasts. Her hair is an abundance of pink curls toppling over one another. Her skin is baby's breath white.

"Good morning," I say, even though it's dark and before midnight. I stand. "You look beautiful."

"Thanks." She leaves the path, walking across the leaves and lawn to me, eyeing the scene before her. "I've never seen anything like this." She moves to kiss me on the lips, but I offer her my cheek instead and, after a moment's surprised hesitation, she pecks it.

Baby Doll15 drops the front of her skirt, puts her hands on her hips, and slinks over to the side a little, sultrily. She straightens up, reverses the way her hands are on her hips, pushes her elbows toward each other slightly, and leans forward a little. "So what is this? What are we supposed to be?"

I know what she means, but I don't feel like explaining the obvious: this is a different time; a time when there was time; we're others; any others; pretending; making-believe anyone has ever been dignified.

"The world," I shrug, retaking my chair. "People." I gesture for her to sit next to me.

Earlier I noted the *natural* elements of the scene include the night, fog, moon, cemetery, hill, the leafless tree, and my raven. I suggested the table, my hot young followers, and I are *unnatural*.

I suppose one might say a *cemetery* is unnatural (let the dead bury their dead), and one (possibly the same one) might say the hot young female followers and I are *natural*. I don't know if it's natural to bury people. We've been doing it for a long time but that doesn't mean it's natural. I only contend the cemetery is (by no means permanent but) a (for now at least) *fixed* element of the scenery. We could move the table around quite easily, and my hot young followers and I could leave at any time. Why do I consider myself and my hot young followers unnatural? I'm not suggesting we're unnatural because we're hanging out in a cemetery. Cemeteries are (generally) full of more interesting conversationalists than your average office building, church, mosque, or synagogue (for example), so it would seem *more* natural to hang out in cemeteries than in your average synagogue, mosque, church, or office building (not that there's any difference). No. I believe my hot young female followers and I are unnatural because I'm a Christian.

"We all heard your screams and moans of dissatisfaction last night, Baby Doll15," comments one of my hot young female followers, smiling. "It sounded like Guy Boy Man displeased the hell out of you."

"Yeah," says Baby Doll15, blushing pink as her hair. "It was quite a disappointment. I was really unhappy the whole time." She turns to me. "Guy Boy Man." She tries to say what comes next but she can't. I think she wants to thank me. She isn't worried about the words she hasn't said. She means them. Necessarily. What she's worried about is how I'll react to those words. It's funny how we censor ourselves. How we cover up our feelings in these elaborate costumes, which take forever to make and just as long to put on, and we force these words, these sounds, to dance around in an absurd way—a complicated, intricate, puritanical 19th-century way—so as to be proper, and never misunderstood, when we all know, deep down inside, we're going to end up naked growling animals screwing each other, or trying to kill each other, later. With the lights on and everything.

"Don't worry about it," I say.

Just then her cell phone rings. She pulls it out and looks at it. "It's my mom," she says, worried. "Wondering where I am."

All my hot young followers make an "aw" sound in unison. "That's so cute," says one of them.

"I remember when *my* mom used to wonder where *I* was," says another, whimsically.

"Is your mom *always* this adorable?"

"What should I tell her?" Baby Doll15 says, looking at me, anxiously. Her phone rings for the third time.

"The truth?" I suggest.

Her shoulders fall. She stares at me. She can't believe I'm serious.

"Some sort of lie?" I offer.

"Be specific," says Baby Doll15, jumpily.

"Tell her now is not a good time," I say, as the white-clad staff walks toward us, bringing our late-night breakfast.

"The truth works!" shouts Baby Doll15. She flips open her phone, says, "Now is *not* a good time," and then she flips it shut. "I'll have to deal with that later," she mutters.

"That's when everybody deals with problems," I say.

N V P F Z

As alluded to earlier, the reason I have a problem saying my hot young followers and I are *natural* is because I'm a Christian. Christians (not me personally) believe homosexuality is wrong because Jesus (is rumoured to have) said so at the (thoroughly *un*documented) last *luncheon*. I don't believe homosexuality is wrong because I don't discriminate, and I think people who discriminate, like Christians, are wrong, but I forgive them because I'm a Christian. Regardless, the main Christian argument against homosexuality is that it's 'unnatural.' Of course homosexuality is *not* unnatural. It happens in nature all the time. Animals are gay. Not all of them, obviously, but the gay ones are. Gay. They'd probably have big fat gay pride parades if they felt compelled to do so because they were openly discriminated against by the other animals, which, interestingly enough, they don't seem to be. When one points out homosexuality *is* [in (actual) fact] natural, Christians are fully prepared for this defeat of their main argument, which makes you wonder why it's their main argument. Christians believe people *aren't* animals. Christians believe people are *better* than animals. Therefore, people are unnatural. I'm a Christian so I believe people are unnatural. (It helps me understand why so many of them discriminate against homosexuals.)

Between the candles, burning straight up in the still night, the white-clad staff lays a bunch of silver (Atomic number: 47; Symbol: Ag) platters, crystal carafes, and golden (Atomic number: 79; Symbol: Au) plates on the long periodic table. (It's a stable table. When I say it's a *periodic* table, I'm not suggesting it's shifting in and out of reality; I'm just saying it has the periodic table of elements on it; and if the table actually *is* phasing in and out of existence, it's doing it so quickly it's imperceptible; in retrospect, I shouldn't have said the table is stable so categorically. How can we know anything is?)

The silver platters on the long periodic table are covered with fresh bread, fresh butter, fresh fruit, and soft cheese. The crystal carafes are filled with milk, cream, orange juice, and apple juice. Champagne bottles in champagne buckets are placed near all of us. Over our heads, the oak's long naked branches reach out for something. The night touches everything the candlelight does not, and even some of what it does. The leaves stay fallen.

Honeydew melon green. Strawberry red. Orange orange.

"Fresh fruit," gasps Baby Doll15. She slides onto the chair next to mine, takes a big handful of purple blueberries, and bites into them. "I can't remember the last time I had fresh fruit. We live in the desert," she explains to the other girls.

The other girls, with their mouths full, nod in understanding.

Even though I picked up Baby Doll15 this morning, and I know her house is in the city, I know what she means about living in the desert.

I pick up a crystal carafe full of cream and pour it over what's left of the blueberries in Baby Doll15's hand; the whiteness slides so easily over what she holds and the sides of her palm.

Baby Doll15 laughs, takes another bite, and moans. "So good."

I marvel at all the small and fleeting variations in her expression, how she says different things to me silently, how she conveys important information about herself, her mood, so easily, all the while staying, unchangingly, moderately to highly attractive. "Eat until you get sick," I encourage.

When presented with a feast, starving people always do the wrong thing. It doesn't matter if they're told, and they understand, it's the wrong thing to do. They do it anyway. The *right* thing to do when you're starving and you have the opportunity to eat whatever you want is to eat just a little. The little you eat should be bland and easy to digest. Then you should wait. Your system needs to get accustomed to food again. After a while, if you haven't gotten sick, you should try to eat a little more. Then you should wait again. You should take it easy for at least a couple of days. From there you can eat progressively more difficult-to-digest food. But starving people never do that. They eat what they've been dreaming to eat, they eat it right away, and they eat as much as they can: ice cream, pizza, chocolate chip cookies, hamburgers, etc. I don't know about you but I have a hard time blaming starving people for doing the wrong thing. In fact, I don't think it *is* the wrong thing.

A little ways down the table, one of my followers holds a champagne bottle. With her perfectly plucked eyebrows up, she looks at me, questioningly, and I smile and nod. She shakes the bottle, holds her thumb over the opening, and directs the spray onto a couple of girls across the table. Each gown these girls wear costs as much as a modest house or an immodest car. It's fun to spend so much money on frivolity when the same money could save other people's lives. They're not *our* lives.

The sprayed girls hold up their hands uselessly against the champagne showering them, close their eyes, and turn away their heads. I can't help thinking that it's what everyone does all the time, but to something far less wonderful than champagne. The girls under attack finally get to their feet and grab champagne bottles of their own. It turns into a war. Except for me, everyone gets involved. I move and stand a safe distance away. The girls can tell I just want to watch. And I do. I want to watch beautiful young women wearing meticulously designed and intricately embroidered gowns spray each with bottle after bottle of champagne until their hair is drenched and pasted down the sides of their face, and their makeup is running like watercolours. I want to watch as they close their eyes, open their mouths wide, and stretch out their tongues, trying to catch those alcoholic raindrops.

Holding up a bent arm to protect herself from the champagne fire, Baby Doll15 runs over to me. "What's the point of all this?" she asks, laughing.

Staring at her happy face, her meaningful eyes, and the way her pink hair is glued in strange ways all over her face and neck, I laugh too. "Exactly," I say.

CHAPTER SIX:
The Living And The Dead

On Monday morning, in the rubble-strewn, water-slick, electric-spark-cracking-and-arcing, blood-splatter-walled, bare-fluorescent-bulb-flickering hallway at Scare City High, after Baby Doll15 and I spent the entire weekend together, despite my better judgement, we're in front of my locker, and it's a night terror. We're kissing, smiling, nuzzling, and whispering! I don't know what the hell is going on! No girl has *ever* had this effect on me! She's taking up so much of my attention, I'm having a hard time smoking cigarettes and drinking whiskey! I'm still doing it, though. I finally figured out the best way to do it. I've got my smoking arm slung around Baby Doll15's shoulders, and when I want a drag, I just kind of get Baby Doll15 in a headlock for a second. She doesn't seem to mind. If I were to sling my drinking arm around Baby Doll15's shoulders, I would've choked the life out of her by now. I take my drinking seriously.

My demons, Mike Hawk and York Hunt, are loving this. They're saying incredibly disturbing things like, "You guys make the cutest couple," and "I knew you two would be great together." My demons usually hiss at girls and call them terribly funny names but they're completely enamoured with Baby Doll15. It's worrisome. Demons are only valuable inasmuch as their advice is contrary to good sense. If a demon suggests a course of action is wise, it's wisest to take the *opposite* course of action. I don't know what to make of their approval of Baby Doll15. All I know is, it can't be good.

Every once in a while, I panic. I think: what am I doing? Why am I still hanging out with Baby Doll15? My demons like her! I should tell her to get lost! But I can't do it! God. What's wrong with me?

The only thing that can reduce your immunity to the bad influence of demons is an angel.

Are angels involved in my feelings for Baby Doll15? I mean, I *do* think she's a little heavenly. Maybe that's why the demons are so supportive. They know what's going on and they're enjoying it. They want to see me suffer. Stupid demons. I *knew* they never liked me. Unfortunately, during the course of exciting adventures I can't be bothered to relate here, I learned it's impossible to track and kill angels. That was, like, one of the first things I tried when I found out how bad they are. They're invincible because everything has to go according to God's plan. [The idea that God is all-powerful, all-knowing, could intervene whenever God wants, and has a plan according to which every little thing goes, but somehow is (miraculously) *not* responsible for anything (or everything) terrible that happens is just angelic propaganda; holy spin.]

Anyway, last Thursday, I informed everyone that it was the final day zombie teachers and zombie students would be permitted at this school. Now, it's Monday morning, after a long weekend. In school, the living kids are trooping in, no longer marching to earn their place in the zombie army, but instead to follow me, in hopes they'll pass through me, leave me behind, and find themselves free on the other side of me, where I'll have their backs. The Zombie Acceptance Test—the ZAT—was scheduled to take place at the end of the week, but now it looks like that's not going to happen, and we're all free. Free to scrounge for survival in a zombie-infested dystopia, as soon as we miss the ZAT. The halls are filled with a nervous excitement.

I'm wearing the Pope's hat, which is a pirate hat, which I pirated, and which I'm wearing; I think I mentioned that already. Covering my breeches and loose-fitting and mostly unbuttoned linen shirt is my ceremonial robe. My ceremonial robe is wrapped around me like all the months in the year. There's no beginning and no end but an infinite number of divisions. My robe is shiny high-tech white. It isn't actually white fabric. It's showing a white image in full HD. I've got my nine-millimetres in their holsters, and I've got my sawed-off pump-action shotgun slung over my shoulder. You never know when a troubled teen, or a group of troubled teens, is going to arrive and start shooting up the school.

While I wait to see how the zombie establishment will react to the banishment of all zombies from the premises, I may (or may not) get a cock fight going. In the eerie flicker of the fallen sky and its faltering fluorescence, a group of students surrounds the flapping, pecking, clawing birds. Money changes hands, forever, staining them, inking their fingerprints, signing everything they touch. A couple of kids have the financial channel on their cell phones; they're observing the cock fight's effect on the stock market.

I'm wagering that the zombie establishment is going to write this school off as a loss and let me and my fellow living human students go about our business. No one intervened after I killed my parents. They must have wanted to avoid drawing attention to me and my cause. The zombie police didn't come after me. I wasn't on the zombie news. Sometimes I think maybe I never killed my parents at all! Anyway, I need to get the world's attention somehow. How can I end human suffering if people don't realize there are zombies everywhere, controlling everything? So far I've only managed to open the eyes of the kids in Scare City High School and, to be honest, I'm not so sure they really believe me as much as they enjoy getting out of class and the thought of missing the ZAT.

"Hey," says Sweetie Honey, walking up to us. On either side of him stand two of his four exotically beautiful, genetically engineered, and behaviourally modified Eastern European girlfriends. He has his arms wrapped around the two girls closest to him, and they, in turn, have their arms around the girls farthest from him, who, in turn, have their arms around the girls closest to him. It moves in and out like that (sexually), over and over. "We caught your sermon on HowToEndHumanSuffering.Com yesterday," Sweetie tells me. "It was great. Thanks for explaining everything to us. And it's so awesome you're the Self-Appointed One. I knew you were a great guy but I never knew *you* knew that too. And really. Thanks for taking it upon yourself to end human suffering."

"Sure."

During yesterday's sermon, I began by telling my fellow (living) high school students what they already knew: Everything is sex. Addition is penetration; subtraction is withdrawal; multiplication is the goal; division is the result. Chemistry, physics, biology: They all spring from and summer in sex; describing it, deriving from it. It's self-fulfilling and self-denying. I asked them, "When are we going to figure out there isn't that much to understand?"

Standing in front of my locker with Baby Doll15,

Sweetie Honey, and his four exotically beautiful Eastern European girlfriends, I watch the living kids walk through the (nightmarish) hallway. I want to believe they're no longer marching into this school to sit idly by while the horrible world that's been willed to them is described in ghastly detail while they take notes. I want to believe they're trooping in to do war with that world. I think back to the way it was, the way it used to be, back in the old days, last week, when zombie teens and zombie teachers ambled around in our very midst. I remember how dead they were. I remember how sick I felt from their rotting stink. I remember all those broken-tooth mouths gaping open and drooling behind their stainless steel muzzles, starving for our brains: the brains of we who remain alive.

"Guy Boy Man!" thunders a thunderous voice. "This is The Principal!" His booming voice cracks and crashes through speakers dangling from the shattered hallway sky. I thought I'd disabled all those instruments of evil by shooting them repeatedly, but now I see someone has put duct tape over the bullet holes and that's fixed them. "Guy Boy Man, I thought you were just kidding when you said teachers and certain students would no longer be allowed at this school but now I can see you're serious!"

"You were a fool to ever doubt my steely resolve, Principal," I say. "Couldn't you tell it was steely?"

"Guy Boy Man! You're expelled from this school!"

"No! This school is expelled from me! Like a turd! I flush you!"

"You can't flush me, Guy Boy Man! I'll be here long after you're gone!"

I frown. "That's gross."

"I won't let you pirate this school, Guy Boy Man!"

"Your days as Principal are done! This is America! We don't tolerate royalty here!"

"He isn't really a prince," whispers Baby Doll15.

"That's what I'm saying," I whisper back.

"This isn't over, Guy Boy Man!" thunders The Principal. Then the crackling speakers go quiet.

"That was The Principal," I explain to Sweetie Honey and his four exotically beautiful Eastern European girlfriends, casually. "He's my enemy. He's pretty much the most powerful person in the school." I shrug. "I'm in the process of destroying him, and it's pretty dramatic."

Yesterday, during my sermon, I insisted that we, living high school students, are smarter now than we'll ever be again, which isn't very smart, because we've been taught the same things that were taught to our zombie parents, zombie grandparents, and zombie ungreat-grandparents, and look what a mess they made of things. Regardless, we, living high school students, are smarter now than we'll ever be again. (Not that smart.) We might not beat our history teacher on a history test, or our math teacher on a math test, but we could almost certainly outperform our math teacher on a history test and our history teacher on a math test. We'd *decapitate* our zombie parents on either test. Now is the time for us to make a stand.

"Hey, Sweetie, I don't think you've met my girlfriend." I tip my head at Baby Doll15. "Look at her. She's got big boobs, doesn't she?" Baby Doll15 is wearing a baby blue baby doll (she wasn't allowed to wear baby dolls when the zombies were in charge of the school. Too sexy. Just one more good reason to get rid of the zombie establishment) over thigh-high white leggings and a pair of baby blue stilettos. "Baby Doll15, this is Sweetie Honey. He's a ninja and pretty much my best friend. Sweetie Honey, this is Baby Doll15. She's got big boobs. I said that already."

Baby Doll15 and Sweetie shake hands and exchange pleasantries, but there's something suddenly awkward about Sweetie, who's normally so cool. He looks rattled, not quite flustered, but out of sorts. For a second I think maybe Baby Doll15 and Sweetie know each other already. Maybe they're having an affair! Maybe they're doing it in every position imaginable, and in a bunch of positions I can't imagine, which Baby Doll15 really likes, and she's just too shy to tell me about, but when I look at Baby Doll15, I can tell she's never met him before. Plus I remember she'd never had sex before Friday morning when she first had it with me. I look at the four exotically beautiful Eastern European girls, who, I've got to say, are an amazing invention on the part of science (although, obviously, I'm waiting for sex robots before I declare the greatest scientific invention of all time) and the girls are frowning at Sweetie, like they're having the same thoughts I had, but slower, obviously, because I'm done thinking about Baby Doll15 and Sweetie and I've moved on to sex robots, which are going to be awesome.

"You're the most beautiful girl I've ever seen," says Sweetie to Baby Doll15, embarrassed.

"Whoa," I say. "She's all right, but come on."

The four exotically beautiful Eastern European girls scowl at Sweetie.

"No I'm serious," says Sweetie. "Most beautiful." He breaks invisible boards in the air. "Ever."

"Thank you," says Baby Doll15, uncomfortable. She clings to me nervously.

I take a slug of my whiskey. "I mean, she's cute, but . . ."

Sweetie keeps staring in awe at Baby Doll15. The four Eastern European girls keep frowning at Sweetie.

"This is like when you bump teeth during a kiss," I note.

"I'm so sorry," says Sweetie to Baby Doll15. "I'm staring. It's just. Hey. These are my girlfriends. Oana, Iulia,

Marta, and Agata. They were genetically engineered and behaviourally modified by diabolical Eastern European scientists."

Suddenly, Sweetie Honey turns and squints coldly down the length of the broken and sporadically lit hall.

I take my arm off Baby Doll15's shoulders. I turn and look in the same direction as Sweetie. I don't see anything in the inconstant and eerie artificial light. However, I trust Sweetie's ninja instincts. I crouch and set down my whiskey bottle. I stand back up, take one last drag, drop my cigarette butt, and grind it on the floor from side to side under my shoe. The cock fight is over. (It sort of mirrors the verbal exchange between The Principal and I.) One bird lies dead. (Metaphorically, The Principal would be the dead bird. Remember when I flushed him? That was awesome.) The other bird pecks at invisible seed on the floor. (I don't know how that pertains to me. Oh, wait.) I stick my hand into the front of my ceremonial robe, and I reach back and put my hand on the reassuring grip of my nine-millimetre. "What is it, Sweetie?" I whisper.

"Troubled teens," he whispers. "Good thing I'm wearing my backpack." He takes it off, sets it down, and starts getting undressed. "A group of forty troubled teens is approaching." Sweetie strips naked quickly. Everyone stares. When he gets down to his incredibly tight briefs, everyone gasps. (He's got a really big penis, in case you forgot.) He probably has to wear incredibly tight briefs to prevent any flopping around because even a sound that (presumably) soft might reveal his position when he's travelling stealthily, which is the only way ninjas travel. Sweetie picks up his backpack, opens it, and pulls out his ninja outfit. He starts getting dressed.

"Forty," I whisper, awed. "So many troubled teens." I let go of the nine-millimetre, opting instead for the pump-action sawed-off shotgun. I take it off my shoulder, pump it, and curse under my breath as an unused shell goes flying. I go over, pick it up, and reload it. "Do you have time to make it to your locker and get your swords and throwing stars?"

"Yes," whispers Sweetie, pulling his ninja hood over his head, and fixing the opening.

Worried, Baby Doll15 grabs my arm. "Guy Boy Man, what are you going to do?"

"Kill." Coldly, I pump the pump-action shotgun again and an unused shell flies out again. I curse louder this time, retrieve the shell and reload it, and peer down the hallway again.

"Guy Boy Man," says Baby Doll15. "Violence is *not* the answer."

I look down the hallway, steely eyed. "Then I don't like the question."

Sweetie and I high five.

"Do you have a match?" I ask him. "I feel like I could light it on my stubble right now."

Suddenly, almost the entire student body is standing behind Sweetie and me, anxiously. There are hundreds and hundreds of them. They're counting on us to protect them from the emotionally disturbed kids that our school psychologists failed to reach, or never knew to reach out to, or were unable to reach because we never had any school psychologists. Almost the entire student body is counting on us to protect them from the kids society failed and that now have to be killed like wild dogs—not that I condone the killing of wild dogs because, surely, if they're offered food and a loving home, they could be domesticated and turned into treasured members of the family.

A long, empty, flickering corridor full of fallen and broken ceiling tiles and spraying pipes and blood-splattered lockers stretches in front of Sweetie and me and, obviously, the hundreds and hundreds of students packed behind us for protection. Silently, Sweetie races to his locker. He undoes the lock and pulls out his weapons. He races back toward us. "You stay here," he tells me. "I'm going to circle around. You just keep them occupied until I get into position. Then, when I'm ready, stop shooting, because you might hit me accidentally."

"I probably won't stop shooting until I run out of ammunition," I admit.

"How much ammunition do you have?"

"Lots and lots."

One of the kids who works in my (alleged) big cock fighting ring is dragging two huge duffel bags to me. One huge duffel bag has loaded magazines for my nine-millimetre. The other has shells for my pump-action sawed-off shotgun.

"Just keep them busy until you see heads getting chopped off," says Sweetie, pushing his way back through the student body. Then he jumps out the window! [All the windows at the school are blacked out (I prefer "opaque") because of troubled parent snipers; that's (one of the several) reasons the hallway is always so dark.] Strangely, when the window breaks, it doesn't make a sound! Ninjas must be trained to jump through windows silently! And, on the way down, they probably grab the broken pieces of glass before they hit the ground! Ninjas are so awesome!

My faithful shoulder-perched raven jumps off me and flies out the broken window, loyally.

"Okay, people," I say, turning to the student body, authoritatively. "It's time to get real. Some of you aren't going to make it. You're going to get shot. If you're lucky, you'll die instantly. If you're unlucky, you're going to writhe around in agonizing pain and then die later. I know this isn't a really upbeat, we-can-do-it speech or anything, but I'm being honest, and I hope that counts for something. Now we need a shield. Something we can hide behind while the troubled kids shoot at us. What can we use as a shield?"

"Fat kids?" suggests somebody.

"That's terrible," I say. "Really. You should never call people 'fat.' 'Overweight,' okay. 'Obese,' fine. Never 'fat.' Good idea, though. Come on. Let's get some heavy kids up front."

The obese and overweight kids step forward, bravely.

"You guys are great," I say, as they pass. "You're heroes. Big heroes. I'm serious." To the others, in explanation, I say, "It isn't cruel, people. It's evolution. Okay, okay. It's cruel but what are you going to do? It's the way things are. We need a human shield and, logically, it makes sense to go with people who're extremely large and a genetic drag on the species."

"I just eat too much and don't exercise," says one overweight kid.

"Don't blame yourself," I say, patting him on the back. "It's genetics."

"I think I could change."

"Well, you couldn't."

He hangs his head and walks to the frontlines.

"Your followers are going to use condoms until they can have vasectomies and tubal ligations," Baby Doll15 reminds me.

"Yeah," I acknowledge. "So what's your point?"

"Their genetics don't matter anymore."

"This is largely symbolic," I confess.

Baby Doll15 tries not to laugh.

"What? Oh. 'Largely'? Yeah. I didn't mean it like that but . . ."

"There aren't enough fat kids to form a human shield!"

cries some guy.

"Overweight," hisses someone else.

I go check it out for myself. When I return, I get close to Baby Doll15. "He's right," I tell her, confidentially. "What the hell is going on? This is America! We should have a wall of flab in front of us a mile thick!"

"Didn't this school get rid of all the sugar-drink and junk food vending machines?"

"Yeah," I say, remembering. "And now we're all probably going to die from the unintended consequences of that misguided decision. First of all, it's un-American. People should be free to eat whatever—"

"You've got to come up with something else," interrupts Baby Doll15.

"Right." I address all the students depending on me. "Are there any special ed. kids here?"

A kid raises his hand, enthusiastically. "I'm a poor reader!"

"Great!"

"I have problems with math!" calls somebody else.

"Terrific! Come on up, you guys! Hey, everybody! Look how excited the special ed. kids are to contribute! What about disabled people? Do we have any disabled people here?"

In the distance, a clearing appears in the students. In the clearing, a girl in a wheelchair tries to, discreetly, wheel herself away.

"Would somebody bring her up here, please?"

She screams and screams. A couple of guys push her to me.

I crouch down in front of her, because that's how you're supposed to talk to people in wheelchairs; they like it when you get down on their level and talk to them eye to eye. They also like it when you sneak up behind them and start pushing them somewhere really quickly because it's like going on an adventure! But now is not the time. (It is but it isn't a *good* time.)

"Listen, wheelchair girl," I say. "I know you're scared. We're all scared."

Everyone murmurs in agreement.

"Do you go to church, wheelchair girl?" I ask her.

"Yes," she says, angrily. Her arms are crossed. Her face is splotchy with emotion. Her legs are withered from disuse. "Why?" she asks.

"Because," I say. "If you go to church, you get to go to Heaven, right?"

"That's not exactly how it works."

"Don't you want to go to Heaven, wheelchair girl?"

"Not right now!"

"Well," I say, nodding, understandingly. "You're going." I stand. "Somebody tie up her hands and push her up with the big ones and the special ed. kids."

"A spinal injury isn't a hereditary condition," she cries when her hands are tied. "I can't pass it on," she calls back as she gets pushed to the front.

"Only the strong survive," I call to her. "Or the heavily armed." I turn to the student body. "No other disabled people? Really? That's disgraceful. I'm sure there are all kinds of disabled kids who'd love to go to school with us. They probably have their own school. They probably just sit around, miserable, wishing they were here with us, doing what able-bodied students are doing. Well, I think we can all say, 'We wish they were here too.' Right now, anyway. They'd probably make us uncomfortable the rest of the time."

A couple of gunshots ring out. Behind me, people start screaming. I wrap, unwrap, and wrap my fingers around the sawed-off pump-action shotgun. I pump it. An unused shell goes flying out. I've got to stop doing that. I stick the butt of the shotgun into my shoulder, ready to blast. I search for targets over the shoulders of the overweight and special needs kids. What I see takes my breath away. Troubled *zombie* teens! Heavily armed troubled zombie teens! They aren't even wearing muzzles!

I turn away. If I wasn't so pale to begin with, the colour would leave my face. Hell, if I wasn't me, I'd leave me too.

"What is it?" asks Baby Doll15, concerned.

I walk over to the lockers, lean back against them, and slide down until I'm sitting on the detritus-covered floor. "Those aren't regular troubled teens," I say, soberly (well, drunkenly soberly). "They're troubled *zombie* teens."

An ungodly moan emerges from the group of zombie teens ambling toward us.

"What did it say?" I ask.

" 'We just want to learn,' " translates Baby Doll15.

I think about that. I roll the words around in my mind. I change their order. I take them apart and examine the words within the words. I rearrange the letters. I see the undelivered. "What if *we're* the troubled teens?" I ask Baby Doll15. "Hey, I can totally see your panties."

"The troubled teens are getting really close," whispers some random dude.

"It doesn't matter," I say. I sigh, getting up and turning to Baby Doll15. "It matters about your panties. It doesn't matter if we're the troubled teens or not. Right or wrong, I've taken a side. My side. They're on their side." I pump the shotgun again. An unused shell flies out again. I clench my teeth, furious. My head shakes in anger for a minute. "The wrong side," I finish. I sling the shotgun over my shoulder, stick my hands into the front of my robe, and I reach back, withdrawing my nines from their holsters. When my hands are reassuringly full of guns, I pull them out, and my robe slips back together in front of me, making the robe seamless.

Most people don't know zombies can use guns. Rigor mortis doesn't last very long. Zombies move stiffly because their lives are so fixedly rigid. They keep their arms stretched out like that because they're searching for something that doesn't exist but believe is just up ahead.

I look over at all the frightened people looking at me, the people I'm protecting. I know some of them think I'm crazy, but they don't care, because I'm not boring. I'm okay with that. I'm willing to stipulate the possibility I'm crazy. I wonder if they're willing to stipulate I could be right. Think about the Earth-isn't-the-centre-of-the-universe guy. Think about the Earth-goes-around-the-sun guy.

Another ghoulish groan emerges from the undead horde ambling toward us. Baby Doll15 translates, " 'Let's talk about this.' "

"The trouble with talk is," I say, pointing my handguns over the shoulders of the overweight and special needs kids, "it doesn't solve anything."

"That's not true," says Baby Doll15.

I squeeze the triggers. Nothing happens. Disappointed, I say, "Baby, please don't say anything *between* the time I say something bad-ass and the time I pull the triggers. It's okay you did it just then because the guns didn't shoot but don't do it again, okay?"

"What if you say something else stupid?"

"Ignore it."

"That's what I usually do."

"Well then, keep doing it."

I turn the guns and look at them. The safeties are on. I click them off. I point the guns at the troubled zombie teens again. "I wonder what my mom's friends are going to think about *this*." I pull the triggers again. Nothing happens

JAMES MARSHALL

again. I mutter curses while I stick one gun in my armpit and chamber a round in the other gun. Then I stick *that* gun in my armpit and I chamber a round in the *first* gun. I point the guns at the troubled zombie teens again and pull the triggers again. The noise and recoil scares the hell out of me. I dance around a little, cursing some more.

Baby Doll15 looks at me, holding her fingers in her ears.

"I didn't think they'd work," I explain.

She nods. "You blew the side of a teenager's head off."

"Was it awesome? I had my eyes closed."

"It was terrible and gross."

"Awesome, then. Just say, 'Awesome.' "

Suddenly the troubled zombie teens open fire! There are so many of them! (Thirty-nine.) It's times like these that I curse America's restrictive gun laws! If only I were allowed to purchase fully automatic weapons (legally)! In front of me, heavy kids start dropping like (enormous, wingless) flies. Baby Doll15 and I hunker down behind a big pile of their bulky bodies. Behind us, the remaining student body lays flat on the rubble-strewn stroboscopic hallway, covering their ears, staring at me, wide-eyed, depending on me to keep them alive (and from becoming zombies), so they can die old and, most likely, miserable.

Emptying my clip, yelling in a way I contend is manly, I blind-fire over the dead bodies of obese kids. The kid who works in my (alleged) big cock-fighting ring hands me fresh clips when I pop out the empties. I slam home the magazines and take a quick look over the bodies. I dropped four more troubled zombie teens with lucky shots. They're writhing around but no longer advancing. I can send them to Hell later (or Heaven if God is forgiving and understanding). I blind-fire again. And again. I empty clip after clip. It's not working. The troubled zombie teens are getting closer and closer. I'm thinning them out, but I'm not stopping them.

N V P F Z

What's taking Sweetie Honey so long? It's time to get creative.

"I need books," I yell. "Thick books."

The student body comes through. Within moments, I have a big stack of thick books. "Somebody tape them to the girl in the wheelchair," I yell.

"What are you doing?" asks Baby Doll15, scared.

"I'm going in," I say, determined.

"Guy Boy Man," she says, horrified, kneeling, sitting on her heels, giving me another look at her panties. "Don't. Please. I . . . I can't lose you."

I pull Baby Doll15 to me and kiss her long and hard and with lots and lots of tongue. "You're not going to lose me here today. Maybe somewhere else. Later on. You never know." I squint at her, glance at her panties, and squint at her again. "That's not true. Sometimes you do."

"I never want to lose you, Guy Boy Man," she says, with tears in her eyes.

I stare at her panties for quite a while. Then I grab my shotgun. A few seconds later, ducked down, I push the wheelchair girl ahead of me with one hand, and with the other hand, I let loose with blast after blast of sawed-off shotgun fire from between her legs. Zombie feet get separated from zombie legs. When the zombies fall, I fire into their heads. The wheelchair girl is riddled with bullets from the troubled zombie teens ahead of us. The thick books taped to her keep the bullets from penetrating her thin-wheelchair-girl body and, more importantly, from hitting me. Unfortunately, nobody taped books to her face, probably thinking it was rude to tape books to a wheelchair girl's face, and that's where she gets shot, a whole bunch of times, pretty much as soon as we set out.

"You're in Heaven now, wheelchair girl," I say, over the deafening roar of gunfire. "I'm sure you'd thank me if you could." As I let loose with blast after blast, hiding behind the dead body of the wheelchair girl, pushing my way forward through the fallen, I wonder if we go to Heaven as soon as we die. Not all of us, obviously. People who haven't accepted Jesus Christ as their lord and saviour don't get to go to Heaven, which is unfortunate, because I (almost always) like (*way*) more of those people than I do people who *have* accepted Jesus as their lord and saviour. But that's neither in between nor off to the side. I wonder if we get to go to Heaven as soon as we die. Jesus is supposed to come back and judge the living and the dead, right? So, when we die, do we just lie in our graves, dead, until he comes back, judges us, and *then* we get to go to Heaven? Or is there, like, some sort of pre-judgement, pre-approval stage, which allows us to go to Heaven until Jesus comes back, judges the living and the dead, returns to Heaven, and then *verifies*, either orally or perhaps in writing, that we, the dead in Heaven, pass muster, and can stay? Or is Heaven totally empty right now and no one gets to go until Jesus comes back and judges the living and the dead? I wish I knew someone who knew, because I'd ask that person.

When I take a quick look beyond the dead wheelchair girl, just as I'm starting to believe I might be able to kill all the troubled zombie teens by myself, I see Sweetie Honey drop from the ceiling. His magnificent sword flashes, slicing through troubled zombie teen after troubled zombie teen. He moves fluidly, wasting no energy, transferring momentum from one kill to the next. He stuns with his (admittedly impressive) body and removes life (or introduces death) with his beautiful sword. Sweetie sidekicks a zombie kid in the chest. The zombie kid flies back, lands on the ground, slides back (farther), and rolls (stiffly) around. As the (floored) zombie kid tries to raise the handgun it managed to hold, Sweetie front-flips toward it. Sweetie lands in the fighting stance over the zombie kid and stabs his sword down into the zombie kid's forehead. Through zombie bone. Into zombie brain. Sweetie withdraws his weapon and ducks down under the M16 that another zombie is holding a foot from his back. Sweetie spins and sweeps that zombie's legs out from under him. The M16 rapid-fires into lockers and then into the ceiling as the zombie falls! That's illegal! That zombie modified a semi-automatic M16 and turned it into a full-auto M16, which you're not supposed to do, because it isn't fair to people who're shooting at you in full accordance with American law! Regardless. Before the fallen zombie can point the M16 at its target again, Sweetie stands over the zombie and stabs his shining sword down into the zombie skull. The point where the sword disappears into skull seems magnified out of all proportion. Pulling out his blade, Sweetie spins and spin-kicks away another troubled zombie teen's outstretched rifle. He forward-snap-kicks the troubled zombie teen under the chin, sending the troubled zombie teen flying up and backwards. The troubled zombie teen freezes, mid-air, at the height of its flight, and then falls, at normal speed, hard. In slow-motion, Sweetie permits himself to fall backwards to the floor. On his way, he lets loose with throwing stars. Five zombie students stand for a moment with throwing stars embedded in their foreheads, before they collapse, no longer undead, but instead dead, which is better.

And then it's over.

Sweetie is back on his feet. He bows respectfully to the fallen students. Then he sheathes his sword and walks toward us.

Sweetie's four exotically beautiful Eastern European girlfriends run to him. They wrap their arms around him, covering his masked face with kisses. "You were so great, Sweetie!" says Oana.

"Actually, I made a lot of mistakes," says Sweetie, pulling off his mask.

"Nobody could tell," says Oana.

"No, I know," says Sweetie. "Only a ninja could recognize my errors." Sweetie walks up to me and shakes my hand. "You did well, Man."

"Thanks, Honey." After a while, I let go of his hand, because I think we've shaken hands long enough, and he seems to want to keep going. "Hey," I say. "Where were you? What took you so long?"

"Oh, yeah. Sorry." He points his thumb over his shoulder. "I ran into someone. A friend. From my old school. I knew you'd be okay so I stopped and talked for a bit." He lowers his hand. "Is that all right? You're not upset with me, are you?"

"No. Of course not. It's cool. I was just wondering. Because you're a ninja, and you said you'd help, and I just had to take on forty heavily armed troubled zombie teens pretty much singlehandedly."

"Right," says Sweetie. "So what'd you think of the fight, Baby Doll15?"

Baby Doll15 has her arms wrapped around me, happily. "I thought Guy Boy Man did amazing," she says, looking up at me proudly. "He killed so many people. Using the wheelchair girl as a form of moving-cover was a stroke of genius."

Sweetie nods for a while. Then he says, "No, I meant about how I did."

"You did well," says Baby Doll15, with a shrug.

"Really? Because I wasn't sure. It felt okay. But you can't always go by that. It's important to get an outside perspective."

The four exotically beautiful Eastern European girls narrow their eyes at Sweetie.

"Yeah, no," says Baby Doll15, holding me tight. "I think you did fine."

"Thanks," says Sweetie. "I appreciate that. And hey. You were really brave."

"I was so worried about Guy Boy Man," she says, putting the side of her head against my shoulder. "I didn't want him to get shot. Not even once."

Sweetie's shoulders fall. "Right."

You can't see what anyone else sees. You can't be them, seeing the same thing. The chances of two people witnessing the same phenomenon and placing it in exactly the same context—categorizing, ranking, or arranging it in whatever ordering system they have in their minds—are about as astronomical as life evolving on the fragments of an exploding grenade. I wonder if Sweetie sees Baby Doll15 the way I saw her initially (cute), or the way I see her now (moderately to highly attractive). Which is the real Baby Doll15?

"Somebody fetch my whiskey and smokes!" I yell.

"Hey, Baby Doll15," says Sweetie, excitedly. "If you had to pick a favourite part, like, of what I was doing and everything, what would it be?"

"I don't know," says Baby Doll15, indifferently. "The throwing stars?"

"Really? That comes so easy to me. Seriously. I can put a throwing star into somebody's eyeball from a hundred yards away on a windy day."

"Great," says Baby Doll15, uninterested.

Hurt and angry, the four exotically beautiful Eastern European girls glare at Sweetie Honey.

"Am I drinking whiskey and smoking cigarettes right now?" I yell. "Because if I am, I can't tell. I only like it when I can tell!"

CHAPTER SEVEN:
When You Get Attacked By A Pack Of Ravenous Wolves, At Least You've Got A Chance

After sending forty heavily armed troubled zombie teens to their second and final deaths at my high school, the zombie establishment leaves me alone for a few weeks. There's nothing about a school shooting on the news. There's no public outrage over the re-deaths of so many young zombies. No angry zombie parents stumbling toward my castle with torches and pitchforks. The zombies cover it up. They bury it. I'm disappointed. I need publicity. How am I supposed to end human suffering if the suffering humans (for the most part) don't even realize they're (always) suffering? I should know better by now.

Zombies control everything. The media is just one of their playthings. Zombies create reality. If they don't want you to know, they don't tell you. If you figure things out for yourself, they produce "experts"—aside from human children, experts are the thing zombies produce most of— and these "experts" have multimedia presentations that (should) prove to you that you're wrong (even though you aren't). If you're still not convinced, the zombies invite you to one of their many zombie institutions for additional help (translation: infection). I'm contemplating when to make my next move when Baby Doll15 makes the decision for me.

She and I have been growing closer and closer. For some reason, I hardly ever want to have sex with any of my followers now. I'm just not into it. My followers don't like Baby Doll15 at all, but they treat her well, because they know I want them to. My demons, Mike Hawk and York Hunt, *love* Baby Doll15. Whenever she isn't around, they remind me about her. They praise her. They extol her virtues. It makes me nervous, but I can't disagree with them. She's amazing. Whenever we're together, I'm happy, and wracking my brains for ways to make her as happy as she makes me, but nothing I buy her, and no place I take her, seems to make her as happy as when she sees me. I don't understand. I can't believe I have the same effect on her as she has on me. It seems impossible. Too good to be true.

I got her a diamond. It was an enormous diamond, but it wasn't enough. So I had the diamond covered with a thick layer of gold. I didn't think *that* was enough, either, so I had the thick layer of gold caked with *more* enormous diamonds. Then I had *that* dipped in gold again. I repeated those steps a few more times. It still wasn't right. Why wasn't it good enough? What was it missing? A ruby layer? I added it. An emerald layer? Stuck them on. A thick coating of platinum? I was never satisfied. By the time it got to the size of a ten-pin bowling ball—big, gold, and studded with huge diamonds—I was so desperate to give her something, anything that might begin to start the infinite journey that a million eternal wanderers would have to undergo (forever) to never find the far-flung reaches of the awkward (mere) representations of my feelings for her, I gave the grotesque and obnoxious thing to her. "I wanted to give you this," I told her. I'd had a thick gold chain and ankle cuff made, and attached to the big gold and diamond ball, so she could drag it around without worrying about losing it.

"A ball and chain," she noted, noncommittally, as I kneeled before her and affixed it to her leg.

"You can see the gold and diamonds," I said, "but there's a bunch of other stuff in there too." I stood up and admired my handiwork.

"Is this a representation of what I mean to you or what you believe you mean to me?"

I tried to make sense of that but I couldn't. "There were so many words in that sentence," I complained.

"Am I burden to you?" she asked, simply.

"Of course not," I scoffed. "Baby, I've got so much money I don't even *notice* you."

She limped away from me, dragging the big gold and diamond ball behind her.

"You're welcome," I called after her.

Now, I'm by myself in the bathroom. I'm not really by myself. No. If I had to metaphorically state my position in regards to myself, I'd say I'm behind me. One hundred percent. But I'm not doing anything dirty. No. In truth, right now, I'm alone in the bathroom, and I'm in front of myself. I'm looking at myself in the mirror, trying to tame my crazy black hair with a diamond comb. The guy who sold me the diamond comb said it would definitely tame my wild hair, but he was a liar! Or else he truly believed it would work and he was merely wrong. He's not my concern. He's the business of the assassins I hired to have him killed in as painful a manner as they could dream up. I really encouraged them to put some thought into it and, as they left, they were already bouncing ideas off each other, so I'm optimistic. I'm combing my hair now because it's wet. And it's not like I'm fresh from the shower.

N V P F Z

I just finished wrestling my demons, and trying to drown them. They were really getting on my nerves. I had Mike Hawk in a headlock, trying to strangle the life out of him. While I struggled with Mike Hawk, York Hunt suggested different (elaborate) scenarios I could orchestrate to tell Baby Doll15 I love her: a romantic stroll on a beach in the Caribbean; she and I sipping espressos at an outdoor café in Rome; space tourism. I filled the bathtub. I stuck Mike Hawk's head under the surface of the water and held it there until Mike Hawk went limp. When I released my demon and stood, Mike Hawk emerged from the water, laughing.

"You can't drown demons," he said.

"You can try," I replied, annoyed.

"Why don't you just tell her?" said Mike Hawk. "Tell her how you feel. That's all you want to do. It's three little words. You imagine yourself telling her, for the first time, a thousand times a day, and you imagine yourself telling her a thousand times a day after that."

"Don't tell me what I imagine," I warned, pointing a finger at Mike Hawk. "You can't even *imagine* what I imagine."

"You believe love is a zombie emotion, right?" said York Hunt. "Well, why does it have to stay that way? Why can't you pirate it and make it human?"

(This was sort of like when Jesus got tempted in the desert.)

"You have trillions of dollars but the only thing you want is to tell Baby Doll15 you love her," said York Hunt. "That's beautiful, good, and important. You should do it."

I tried to drown York Hunt too, but that didn't work either.

Anyway, now, I open the mirror (not the layers of it;

rather the cabinet it conceals) to put away my diamond comb after having accomplished nothing with it. When I close the mirror, Baby Doll15's unicorn is standing behind me, looking at me in the mirror over my shoulder. It's startling. In a brave manner that bespeaks of my calm in a crisis, I jump around for a while, wide-eyed, slapping at the air, cursing mightily. Then I turn to the unicorn behind me in the bathroom, and say, coolly, "Hey, unicorn. You startled me."

The unicorn snorts.

"So what's up?"

The unicorn doesn't say anything. That doesn't surprise me. So far the unicorn hasn't said anything to me. I don't think it's said anything to anyone else, either. It might not be a talking unicorn. It might be a mute. Perhaps it received some sort of horrible shock when it was a young unicorn. Perhaps it needs someone to help it overcome its trust issues. If it does, it should try elsewhere.

"If you're trying to communicate with me telepathically," I tell the unicorn, "it's not going to work." I tap my finger against my temple. "No unauthorized access."

The unicorn looks at itself in the mirror. Then it looks at me. I look in the mirror and see the unicorn. The biblical beast turns and leaves the bathroom.

"Do you want me to follow you?" I call after it.

Whether it wants me to or not, I follow it. It turns a corner at the end of the hallway. When I get there, and turn the same corner, the unicorn is gone. "Okay if you still, or ever did, want me to follow you, you've gone some place I can't go now," I yell. "And possibly not even later on, either."

Baby Doll15 enters the hallway in front of me, where the unicorn disappeared. "Who are you talking to?" she asks.

"Your unicorn," I say. "Actually it might not have been

yours. It might have just looked like yours. It was a unicorn, though. If you want me to get all metaphysical on you, it might have been a hologram, a robot, or a hallucination."

"I'm the only one here," says Baby Doll15.

"You haven't seen your unicorn?"

"Not lately."

"Are *you* the unicorn?" I ask, suddenly suspicious.

Baby Doll15 laughs. "You've seen us together, Guy Boy Man."

"Maybe the unicorn is a physical manifestation of your impressiveness, elusiveness, and, according to non-believers, illusiveness."

"I'm right here," she says, holding up her arms. "You can have me."

"That's true," I admit, still slightly suspicious.

"I'm real," she says. "And I'm not going to run away."

"Okay," I say. "Yeah. Of course, yeah. You're right."

I pretend my fears are assuaged, but they're not. They're worse now. Stupid fears. Why do they always have to be so scary? I miss the old days when all you had to worry about was where your next meal was coming from, and how to stay dry and warm, and if any wild animals were going to attack you in the night. All the stuff I worry about is so cerebral. When you get attacked by a pack of ravenous wolves, at least you've got a chance. There's no escape from the brain.

CHAPTER EIGHT:
Hurting People Is Hilarious

I love you, I love you, I love you.

I can't say it. If I say it, I'll lose all my money. That's the deal I made with Centaur111.

When Baby Doll15 and I are talking and laughing, when we're walking in silence, when we're happy from being together and flushed with our proximity and smiling because we can't help it, and looking away from each other self-consciously, when we're both feeling exactly the same, I can't say it. The words are anathema to me. (That means bad.) They're poisonous. Even though I feel their effects, I can't go back to their cause. I had no idea being this ecstatic could be so wretched. When I look at Baby Doll15, euphorically hurting in parts of my heart and mind I didn't even know existed, I know it has to end.

"Where are we going?" asks Baby Doll15, walking out of the castle, followed by her unicorn. Baby Doll15 is wearing an orange baby doll—it clashes with her pink hair—over pink leggings—the baby doll clashes with her leggings too—and orange high heels, which clash with her hair and leggings. The outfit is complimented by me—"Hey, I like your outfit." "Thanks."—and complemented by a sparkly silver handbag, which reflects the heavenly peace of her eyes. Her shiny thick hair is curled into perfectly spiralling double helixes.

I hold out her bomb disposal suit. "We're going to prison." I'm already wearing my bomb disposal suit over my usual ceremonial robe, layered over my pirate outfit and guns. My pirate hat—the Pope's pirate hat—is already inside the enormous mining bulldozer.

"I don't want to go to prison," whines Baby Doll15, stopping, crossing her arms. The unicorn stops next to her.

I lower the bomb disposal suit, surprised. "Why not? What's wrong with prison?"

"It's depressing."

"No, it's not. It's great. Come on." I tip my head at the bulldozer. "You'll love it. I'll buy you some cotton candy."

She sighs, letting me help her into the bomb disposal suit.

There's no way this can last. The words must be spoken. Sooner or later. They become necessary. The feeling, sense, and sentiment must be expressed. What starts as, more or less, nothing becomes, less or more, something, and there's, seemingly, no need to discuss or document the lack of it (i.e., specifically, see, read, "love"), when, in point of fact, that may be more worthy of investigation, but regardless, the development of love is much like finding yourself at the top of a slide with someone else, and suddenly, without reason, both of you spill down the slide until you hit the ground. The two of you have to get up, dust yourselves off, and either say, "Ouch," or "That was fun," because there was a slide there, and you both went down it, whether you intended to or not. You can't ignore it. You can't just go your separate ways without discussing what happened.

It only takes us ten minutes to get to a prison. This is America. We pull up outside. Muzzled zombie parents are walking in and out of the maximum-security facility, holding hands with their still-human children, who're eating candied apples and clutching the strings of helium-filled balloons. Overhead, a big neon sign scrolls and flashes: "Open to all ages!"

"I'm telling you right now," says Baby Doll15, as I easily crash and smash four SUVs and three mid-sized sedans out of my parking spot, "I am *not* going to the showers."

"Okay."

"Really?"

"Whatever you want, Baby." I help her out of the bulldozer. Her gold and diamond ball and chain tumbles down after her, banging once harmlessly into the backs of her bomb disposal suit-covered legs and then down onto the ground.

"Here comes your unicorn," I say, awkwardly lifting my arm, encased in the bomb disposal suit, pointing out the animal, running down a rainbow that ends in the parking lot nearby.

"It's not my unicorn," she insists.

Watching it walk toward us, I marvel at its beauty, its grace and elegance. I watch its massive muscles move under its glowing white skin. I stare at its white mane and tail, moving with the wind it creates with its purposeful stride. If pride is a sin, this unicorn should be forgiven. But forgiveness is a slippery slope.

Tumbling down the important and meaningful slide, like Baby Doll15 and I did, is an event. When you get to the bottom of it, certain questions must be answered. Certain decisions need to made: Did you both intend to go down the slide? Whether you did or not, did you both enjoy it enough to forget any reluctance or unwillingness? Did you like it enough to justify climbing the ladder again? If not, how do you say you've had enough without hurting your playmate's feelings, or are you the kind of person who only thinks of your own enjoyment? If you aren't, are you willing to sacrifice your own happiness for the continued happiness of your friend? If you won't, how badly should you feel for the disappointment you cause and for how long? Worse, what if you enjoyed it but your partner didn't, and says so, or seems to have not, but says otherwise? Do you try to persuade him or her? Or do you put his or her feelings ahead of your own, and turn trembling away, with a tear trickling down your rosy cheek, and face the rest of the day on your own? It's such complicated fun, isn't it?

After we take off our bomb disposal suits, Baby Doll15 and I walk to a hot dog stand in front of the prison. After we place our orders, and Baby Doll15 gets hers filled, the vendor takes my wiener in his sanitary gloved hand. He holds my wiener in his sanitary gloved hand for quite a while. Then he slides it into a bun and hands it to me. He's got a white hot-dog-vendor hat. It's not a pirate hat, but it's pretty cool.

I'm American so I love the prison system. I wish it were more cruel and unusual, though. Also, I wish it weren't so systemically prejudiced. It discriminates against straight people. (The prison system is Club Med for homosexuals who love discipline and routine.) It also discriminates against the innocent, forcing them to commit crimes if they want to gain admittance, and it discriminates against the guilty, preventing them from paying taxes and doing things like listening to their children crying.

Nearby, kids are getting their faces painted. Some guy holding a stack of thick books is walking around, yelling about how we need to buy our programs, without our programs we won't know who we're looking at or what they've done, they'll just look like regular people sitting in a jail cell, and we won't know what names to call them or why we should be infuriated with them. I wave him over and buy a couple.

It might interest you to know that prisons aren't full of zombies. They're full of living people. Ninety-five percent of the prison population is mentally ill. (Too irrational, irresponsible, and unpredictable to become zombies.) It's obvious that none of these [usually poor (black) people] would've ever committed the crimes for which they were convicted, if they'd received proper medical treatment, or if the proper medical treatment existed, or if they'd been raised in loving homes, or if their loving homes hadn't been located in furiously angry neighbourhoods, or if they had any good luck whatsoever. The five percent of the prison population that *isn't* mentally ill is actually *very* mentally ill. They'd need around-the-clock medical care. That'd cost a lot. [It's cheaper to let innocent people get killed, and to house, clothe, and feed the killers afterwards, because there's usually a really (financially) inexpensive period when the killers are growing up and struggling (alone or among friends and family) with their dysfunctional minds.] Roughly thirty percent of the entire prison population is actually *innocent* of the crimes for which they were convicted, but they're still mentally ill, and there's nowhere else to keep them so cheaply.

Baby Doll15 and I are leafing through our programs and enjoying the last of our hotdogs when suddenly we're attacked by a roving gang of vegetarians! The scrawny vegetable-lovers slap at us, weakly. In a serious state of non-panic and mild discomfort, Baby Doll15 and I hunch up our shoulders and move around, trying to keep our backs to the violent vegetarians, groaning annoyed things like, "Come on," and "Cut it out," and "You're going to knock off my pirate hat, you ugly, misguided, vegetarian slut." That last one was me in case you were wondering.

All of a sudden, the unicorn attacks! It gores the vegetarians! It really concentrates on their private parts! The bumper crop of blood gushes onto my ceremonial white gown, my face, and pirate hat! Bright red bucketsful of vegetarian ooze showers onto Baby Doll15's face, hair, and baby doll! It even coats her high heels! It's kind of hot!

"Jesus," I say, when it's finally over, flicking my soaked hands down while leaning forward so blood drips off my face onto the ground. I don't want to get it on my ceremonial gown, even though the redness beads and dances away (like water off a waxed car) from the high-tech fabric. Interestingly, it doesn't stain the Pope's hat, either. "Why are vegetarians so in-your-face? Are they hanging out in Africa, slap-attacking lions for eating gazelles?"

"I don't know," says Baby Doll15, fingertip-picking her soaked outfit away from her skin.

"That unicorn sure looks after you," I observe.

"Yeah," she says, looking down at what she's doing. "Maybe too much."

The white unicorn is pink as Baby Doll15's hair. Its coat is divided into millions of wet Vs where the wetness pulls hairs together. The unicorn is male. Now, covered in the blood of its victims, it looks feminine. It looks like love.

I'm glad I fell down the slide with Baby Doll15, and I want to tell her I enjoyed it, and I want to do it again, again and again, forever, but I can't say so. I keep hoping she'll let me keep spilling down the slide with her, and we won't have to talk about it, but I know, sooner or later, we will, and the idea strikes such fear in me, I realize I've never known fear before, and the thought of hurting her disgusts me to the point that I recognize I've never felt true disgust before—and I've seen a lot of gross (translation: awesome) stuff, and I thought I was completely desensitized, but maybe it wasn't that I thought so much as hoped (foolishly)—and I keep trying to think of some way around it, some loophole in the law of love that the team of lawyers in my mind can help me wiggle through, but conviction seems unavoidable. I will be sentenced.

After Baby Doll15 and I wipe the blood from our eyes, we walk toward the prison. A muzzled zombie couple ambles toward us, leaving the prison with their arms outstretched toward us, like they want us, which they do, obviously, because they're zombies and they want to eat or infect Baby Doll15 and me because she and I are living people, but for a moment I get the sense that their arms are stretched out toward us for another reason, but I don't know what it is. The zombie couple accompanies their still-human son. He's a cute little guy, probably four or five years old. He's eating a candy apple, taking great big bites of that sweet treat.

When we get close enough, I tell the kid, "Your parents are zombies and they spend every day making the world a horrible place for you to live in, and then one day they're going to bite you, probably when you're not even paying attention, so you become a zombie too, and then you'll live in eternal undead torment, and you'll have to eat human beings to survive, just like your parents, and you'll have to find an ugly zombie wench like your mom here and you'll have to do gross, terrible, and disgusting things to her to feed her, to kill her other hunger, so she pukes up babies that you can turn into even more zombies."

The kid starts crying. He holds up the candy apple like it's the Olympic torch and runs away. His parents stumble after him, mindlessly.

"Nice, Guy Boy Man," says Baby Doll15, shaking her head. "Nice."

"It's the truth, isn't it?"

My conviction. My prison. I'll be sentenced because of my inability to utter the only sentence I want to scream at the top of my lungs into the ears of every living and dead, sentient and thoughtless, animal, vegetable, and mineral in every world, real or imagined: I love you, Baby Doll15. And if I were allowed more than one sentence, I'd use them all. It's sick how much I love you, Baby Doll15. In a ritualistic Christian kind of way, I want to eat your body and drink your blood and somehow become you, seeing me, so I can love myself as much as I know you do, and I want you to do the same to me, so you can see how much I love you, more, I know, than you love yourself, so much more, it's impossible that I can like you when I love you this much, because I hate you for not looking after yourself as well as I would, and for getting involved with the dislikes of me, because I hold you, tightly, in so much higher esteem than you hold yourself. I'd be a princess, a queen, an angel, if I were blessed enough to be myself inside you, and perhaps, in a glowing white gown, with solar wind pressing the silk to your skin, floating it away into the cold night of everywhere you aren't, looking into a mirror in Heaven, you could see yourself as I do, as I see you, and you'd know how much you mean to me, and if I had eternity, I'd give it all to you to keep torturing me, and if I had infinity, I'd use every bit of it to torture you right back.

Inside the prison, Baby Doll15 and I stop in front of a cell where you can throw softballs at an embezzler. Three for a hundred bucks. I give the prison guard a thousand dollars. He looks from side to side, nonchalantly. Then he sticks the money into his back pocket.

"What's to stop him from throwing the balls back at us?" asks Baby Doll15.

"Daily beatings," says the guard, nodding. He must get the question a lot. "For the most part it's the daily beatings, but there's also the substandard food. The whole institutional feel of the place tends to wear down the spirit after a while. Plus, I've got Mace, a baton, and a gun. If you want, I can show you how I beat a prisoner. My technique is flawless. Everybody says so."

"Sounds good," I say, turning to the still-bloody version of Baby Doll15. "What do you think?"

"I don't want to see that."

The prison guard and I exchange looks. Women. They're lucky they're hot and have vaginas, breasts, and nice tight asses. Otherwise, evolution would've deselected them a long time ago.

I launch softballs at the prisoner, who cowers on his bunk, covering his head with his arms. Most of the balls bounce back off the bars.

"You've got to hit him *three* times to get a stuffed animal," says the guard.

"This game sucks," I declare, walking up to the bars. "It's rigged." I demonstrate with my last softball. "Look. The balls barely fit through the bars."

"Got to make it challenging," shrugs the guard. "Don't be sore, though. You only got to hit him one more time to win your girl a stuffed animal."

It's funny how words can make your heart ache, your heart break, sometimes. "Your girl." Those symbols and sounds are so important to me right now. I want to hold onto them. I want to keep them. You can't, though. You can't save words. They go bad.

I throw the last ball and hit the embezzler right in the

arm he's using to cover his head. "Did you see that?" I say, turning to Baby Doll15, excited. "I got him right in the arm he's using to cover his head!"

"I saw it," says Baby Doll15, unimpressed.

"Wait until I tell all the hot young girls hanging out in my castle! Nobody is going to believe it! Damn it, Baby. You should've been recording it on your phone!"

"Don't worry," she says, coldly. "They'll believe it." She turns away from me. "People will believe anything."

The prison guard hands Baby Doll15 a big stuffed lion. It's probably full of stuffed gazelles.

"I don't want it." Baby Doll15 passes it to me, like she's disgusted by it.

"Good, because I didn't want to give it to you," I lie, jerking it away. "Come on. Let's go throw darts at a car-jacker."

I'm caught. This is happening sooner than I thought. Having had no experience in this matter up until this point, I could only guess: How long would it take? How long could Baby Doll15 and I go with things so intense between us before the words would become absolutely necessary? Forget the sex, never mind the kissing, ignore the touches, pay no attention to our fingers intertwined, and overlook our staring at each other. Our casual glances would bring blushes to hardcore porn stars. To those not involved, it must seem so ordinary. Perhaps to the followers of my religion it seems *pathetically* ordinary, like a neurochemical response to a biological imperative: to find a mate, reproduce, and pass on my DNA, half of it at least and, sadly, at most, which is *desperate* to get away from me, to try a *new* combination, *anything* new, only to keep failing. But to me and, I believe, to Baby Doll15, it seems like something so special, so important, so extraordinary, nobody in the world could've possibly felt anything like it before. If they had, certainly all the world's problems would be solved by now and everyone would be living in harmony. I know what's happening. I know my mind is tricking me, fooling me into continuing (life), deluding me into misbelieving there's hope, but despite this knowledge—no, stronger than that, this certainty—that this is, in point of fact, what's happening, I don't care at all. Reason is gone. There's only emotion.

Angrily, Baby Doll15 and I walk through the prison's cement and steel. Without looking at me, Baby Doll15 asks, "Do you honestly think your religion is what's *best* for the world?"

"Of course," I answer, without hesitation. "Destroying the world is obviously what's best for it."

We walk in silence for a few moments. "In silence" is a little misleading. There are prisoners howling in pain and humiliation, and children screaming and laughing and running around, and zombies groaning and that kind of thing. We pass the Spin-A-Ponzi-Schemer and the Come-On-Everybody-Let's-Fry-This-Guy. I'm just saying, Baby Doll15 and I don't say anything.

Suddenly Baby Doll15 stops and insists, "There's no such thing as zombies, Guy Boy Man."

I stop too. "Of course there is. They're everywhere. They control everything." Playfully, I move the stuffed lion toward her, like it's going to get her. I'm trying to make peace here.

She ignores it. It's like she's been holding back these words for a while now. "I'm going to take the Zombie Acceptance Test, Guy. Unless you can make some kind of commitment to me and convince me we're going to be together for the rest of our lives, I'm not going to

128

give up on my education. I mean, I'll drop out and become a waitress if we're going to be together, but I really want to take the test if we're just going to break up in a month or two."

I lower the lion. Is she saying that she won't take the ZAT if I tell her I love her? "Baby, you know we're going to be together forever."

She takes my hand in hers. We hold the lion together. Neither of us says anything for a long time. Then Baby Doll15 sighs and says, "Why don't you get into politics and try to change things that way?"

My shoulders fall. "The problem with democracy is that the majority of people are idiots."

"If you think they're idiots, why do you want to help them?"

A billion different thoughts rush through my mind all at once, and I don't know which to focus on, and I don't know if any of them are right, if none of them are, or if all of them are, somehow, even the contradictory ones.

"I want to help people by destroying them," I say.

"If people stop reproducing," says Baby Doll15, "you're going to run out of hot young female followers."

"Sex robots," I say. "Nice try, though. That was a big concern. Come on." I reach out to her. "Let's have fun."

Past the Dunk-a-Drunk-Driver and the Throw-Rings-Around-The-Neck-Of-A-Guy-Who-Accidentally-Killed-Some-Other-Guy, we get to the Car-Jacker Dart Throw. I buy a bunch of darts and offer some to Baby Doll15. She shakes her head.

I throw dart after dart. Most of them miss but quite a few stick. When I get him, the car-jacker curses and jumps around and pulls out the darts as quick as he can. I laugh every time that happens. Hurting people is hilarious.

CHAPTER NINE:

The Ultimate Symbol Of Your Wealth, Power, And Your Love Of Jesus

I have to hurt Baby Doll15. In hurting her, I'll hurt myself. I don't want to. I don't want to do either. If I *never* have to say the necessary words, and if I hadn't *already* taken steps to prevent ever impregnating anyone (I got a vasectomy), I'd stay with Baby Doll15, and I'd give her as many children as she'd like. No matter how strongly I believe—no, no matter how much I *know*—it's wrong to reproduce. I'd do anything to make her happy. And I know it'd make her happy.

She made a passing remark. She envisioned herself one day pushing her children on swings. It was simple for her. The idea made her happy, so she wanted to realize it.

Right now I don't care that she'd, inevitably, love and devote more time to these strangers than she would to me. I'd do it, if I hadn't already taken steps. I'd fertilize the egg of her desire for more than me. Despite her selfishness. Despite her thoughtlessness. Despite her failure to consider, in any meaningful way, the pain, struggle, and stress she and I would have to endure—she'd have to endure it more than I would, obviously, because I'd get an office and start spending a lot of time there—and the impossible decisions we'd have to make, to transform these selfish, slavering, screaming beasts after they emerge from her vagina—that's my vagina, and you're wrecking it!—into socially acceptable and responsible people, or, to put it more precisely, mindless, flesh-eating *zombies* dedicated to, and intent upon, ruining everything for everyone in the course of satisfying their own base desires, bouncing from stimuli to stimuli with no coherent thought for the future or any understanding of their own purpose, other than to bring more zombies into (human) being, to keep dividing, to continue the failure.

This is where it ends.

Baby Doll15 and I are on my pirate ship. It's a state-of-the-art, nuclear-powered aircraft carrier. It's named Industry. Technically I'm unqualified, but everyone calls me "Captain." My aircraft carrier is in port. Moonlight shines off the deck and fighter planes. Baby Doll15 and I are wandering around the high-tech killing machines, holding hands and swinging our arms, happily.

When I got the aircraft carrier, I had to agree not to get fighter planes. When I got the fighter planes, I had to agree not to put them on my aircraft carrier. (I also had to agree not to purchase air-to-air missiles, air-to-ground missiles, cluster bombs, etc.) When I got the munitions, I had to agree not to load them. Kindly, the people who sold me the munitions showed my crew how to load them *hypothetically*.

I don't know if you know this about aircraft carriers, but when you buy one, you get an amazing deal on all kinds of cruisers, destroyers, and submarines to protect it!

Nearby a group of my followers is gathered. The hot young pale-skinned girls wear ridiculously high high-heels in which they manoeuvre with bored ease, black leggings that slightly obscure their shapely calves, knee-length skirts made out of a million layers of crinkly black tulle sticking way out to the sides (making it appear their legs are growing out of upside-down dead and dried carnations), and corsets of various bright colours. Orange, blue, green. Their makeup is severe. Some have their pouting lips done in the same colours as their corsets. Others have their eye shadow done in big black designs. Their hair is spooky, ghost-like, teased back and then sprayed up in a messy kind of way. All my followers hold tall thick white candles that glow yellow near their flapping flames.

"I've got something to tell you," says Baby Doll5, looking down, kicking at something invisible with one of her stilettos. She's wearing a grey baby doll, black leggings, and black high heels. "I think it's appropriate that I tell you here on your aircraft carrier, because it's the ultimate symbol of your wealth, power, and your love of Jesus."

"Jesus preached socialism and pacifism," I say, "which is wrong and un-American, since it discourages entrepreneurship and doesn't support our troops, but I'm a Christian, so I forgive him."

"Are you happy?" asks Baby Doll15, staring down at that which supports us.

"Right now? Yes. Very much so. You?"

"Yes." She says it very seriously.

I can hardly see her in the darkness.

"I've got something to tell you," says Baby Doll15, brushing all her pink hair over to one side of her head with her free hand, turning, and looking at me in the gloom.

"You said that already."

"I'm scared," admits Baby Doll15.

It's strange. No matter how long Baby Doll15 and I hold hands, they never get sweaty. "I thought you said you were happy."

"I am. I'm both. I'm scared about what I've got to tell you, but I'm happy I'm here. Okay, I'm not happy I'm here but I'm happy I'm anywhere with you." We're still strolling in the moonlight shining on the aircraft carrier.

"Maybe you shouldn't tell me," I say, worrying now too.

"I have to."

"Are you sure? Sometimes it's better to put things off. You might not really want to tell me. You might feel like you *have to*, but you don't. It might be one of those things you feel like you've got to do, but then you don't, and the next day you're really glad you didn't."

"It's not one of those things," she says, suddenly confident.

"How do you know?"

"I feel it."

"You can't know a feeling."

"I love you," she says.

I let go of her hand.

She reaches after it for the smallest, most heavily divided fraction of a second, but she catches herself and stops. She stops walking. She stops dead, so dead, in her invisible tracks.

I walk a few more steps. Then I stop too. My back is to her. After a minute, I turn. They say actions speak louder than words but they don't. I don't know if they ever do or never do but when someone says, "I love you," it doesn't matter how many heroic feats you've performed, or impossible problems you've solved, to prove, beyond a shadow's doubt, you feel the same. You have to say it. Verbally. Orally to aurally. With words. Or everything you've done or could ever do doesn't and will never matter.

I don't say anything. I give her more actions to make up for my lack of words. I stare at her, at her eyes, into them, the everlasting peace of them in the aircraft carrier night, with my hands open, silently pleading for what I want: more. So much more. Always more. Like the richest baron or the poorest artist. Nevertheless.

Baby Doll15 looks at me, waiting. She doesn't gasp. She doesn't take a step away from me, like she's just realized she's wrong, or she's right but she's wrong about me, and if she was wrong about me, how could she be right? She doesn't do anything. She just waits, looking at me.

I wait too.

We both stand there, waiting for something that never happens. We wait for something that can't happen. We wait and wait and wait. We wait forever.

CHAPTER TEN:
Nobody Can Ever Get Me

I don't know where Baby Doll15 goes. She disappears. I
don't know how she gets there. I don't take her. When I
return to my castle, as soon as the heavy doors are opened,
I see the gold and diamond ball and its gold chain waiting
on the floor. I don't want it, but as everyone watches, I pick
it up and carry it away. When I'm on the stairs, the chain
slips away from me. It makes a loud cracking sound when it
hits stone. I don't try to pick it up. Instead, I drag it, rattling
and clanking, behind me. It's my ball and chain. It always
was. I gave it to her but it was mine. It was my attachment
to her. It was my burden. All the hot young girls watch me,
wordlessly, as I carry it away. It's weird how you can feel
people watching you sometimes.

The next day in school, there's a note sticking out of
my locker. Who passes notes? It's so *analog*. I pull it out,
unfold it, and read it: "Guy Boy Man, this isn't working. We
need to talk. Baby Doll15." It's the first time I've seen her
writing. It's terrible. How could I ever love someone with
such terrible handwriting? Dramatically, I crumple the
note in my clenching fist. Then, less dramatically, I smooth
it out on my leg, fold it back up along its lines, and stick it

in my pocket. I pull out my cell phone. I text her: "It's over. There's nothing to talk about. It was fun. Say 'Bye' to your big breasts for me."

My followers and I still go to school, even though there are no teachers. That's not accurate. There are no *zombie* teachers. Now, all classes are sex ed. They're very hands on. I'm uninvolved. The Principal is thoroughly engaged. His disembodied voice booms from the dangling intercom speakers constantly. He chastises the young and playful with the strongest words, in the strongest tones: what they're doing is wrong, shameful; what they're doing is dangerous, even when done safely. Right now I don't care about his disinformation.

Shortly after reading the note, feeling its weight in my pocket, still in the hallway, I start sobbing, but in a very masculine way. If any hot young girls see me sobbing, I can't tell through the sad blur, but if they do, I'm sure they're very aroused by the manliness of my grief. Between shaky intakes of breath, I suck on a cigarette and drink whiskey.

Sweetie Honey appears in the broken hallway. All the lockers are painted with a fresh coat of blood. [I had all the heavily armed troubled zombie teens shot in the head yesterday. (I'd already dispatched most of them single-handedly yesterday, but some of them were just seriously wounded and, if you're thinking about getting in the zombie eradication business—it's a burgeoning field with lots of employment opportunities—even when you're really confident a zombie is un-undeaded, or redeaded, you want to be completely sure.) After having them shot in the head, I also had the (formerly) heavily armed (once) troubled (previously) zombie (at an earlier time) teens' bodies cut into pieces, their pieces removed and lit on fire, and their ashes scattered widely]. Sweetie is wearing an all-red pair of sneakers, white sweatpants, a dark blue sweatshirt covered with white stars, and his backpack containing his ninja outfit. Noticing my despair, Sweetie rushes up to me, wraps his muscular arms around me, and cries, "Oh, Guy Boy Man! What's the matter? What's wrong?"

"Baby Doll15 and I just broke up," I weep, stoically.

Sweetie seems to hesitate for a second, but maybe I'm wrong.

I stipulate the possibility I could be wrong. You don't get that with the leaders of other organized religions.

Without letting go of me, Sweetie Honey leans back and looks at me with a sympathetic pout. "It really hurts?"

"No." I shake my head. "It's not like I—" My face scrunches up. I nod. "Okay yeah. It really hurts."

"Oh, Man," he cries, pulling me close again. "It's going to be all right. You've always got me, okay? Not literally. I'm a ninja. Nobody can ever get me. I'm just saying. We'll be best friends forever and who knows, maybe now . . ."

"Maybe now, what?" I ask, when he lets that sentence trail off.

He hesitates again. "We could . . . hang out more?"

"I guess," I sob.

"Guy Boy Man," he says, leaning back and looking at me again. "I know you and Baby Doll15 were close, but it's over now, right? You've got to move on. There are plenty of fish in the sea. Not literally. There used to be. Now there's pollution and over-fishing, so there aren't plenty of fish in the sea. That was a bad analogy."

"I know what you're trying to say," I say, and sniff.

"Good," says Sweetie Honey. He lets go of me and steps back. He claps me on the shoulders, squeezes them, and shakes me a little. "So do you mind if I ask her out?"

"Who?"

"Baby Doll15."

He turns away from me. He starts spinning his combination lock back and forth. He opens his locker. When the door swings open, I look at the pictures of the shirtless hunks stuck to it.

"Why do you have pictures of shirtless hunks in your locker?" I ask. "Are they ninjas too?"

"No," he laughs. He takes off his backpack, opens it, and starts yanking out textbooks and slamming them inside his locker. "They're. Uh. My inspiration. You know. For when I'm training. They. Motivate me."

"That's cool, I guess."

"So what do you say? Do you mind if I ask her out?"

I want to say, "Yes, I mind." I want to say, "I can't believe you're even asking me." I want to say, "I'm going to reach back, grab one of my nines, chamber a round, click off the safety, stick the muzzle against your forehead, and pull the trigger," but I know better than to threaten a ninja, or to even *think* about (actually) killing a ninja. I was only *considering* the *idea* of *threatening* a ninja, which I knew was foolish before I even began thinking it, and I dismissed the thought before it was fully formed, and I only went through the motions of the notion because it'd be rude to interrupt myself. "If that's what you want to do," I say, "you should do it."

"Terrific!" Sweetie Honey makes a fist. He shakes it a little.

Sweetie didn't realize it then, or if he did, he didn't let it show, but he and I had just stopped being friends. We'd started being enemies. And he was a ninja. Obviously, he realized he was a ninja then. When you're a ninja, you never stop realizing you're a ninja. I'm just saying. The fact he's a ninja was something *I* was taking into account more so now that we were enemies.

CHAPTER ELEVEN:
Satin, Silk, And Lace

After school, after Baby Doll15 and I break up, and after Sweetie Honey tells me he's asking out Baby Doll15, my hot young female followers try to cheer me up. They're dressed like wealthy librarians (that's redundant—all librarians are wealthy. They're communists—wealthy communists. Government-protected gangsters, stealing the products of the hardworking poor and renting out those products to the crass unwashed masses for a salary the likes of which the peasants they exploit can only dream). The hot young girls wear designer pencil skirts and tailored blazers. Their hair is pulled back in tight buns. Horn-rimmed glasses complete the look.

"Do you remember the time you put your manhood in a bowl of milk and asked us if we wanted some groin-ola?" asks one of them, laughing.

I'm looking at their outfits, thinking about what's underneath. I'm always thinking about what's underneath. I never get to what I want. It's always buried a little bit deeper. I'm tired of digging. There's lingerie under these girls' outfits. I don't need to see it to know. Red, orange, and yellow. Black, grey, and white. Satin, silk, and lace. It reminds me of Baby Doll15. Baby dolls are a kind of lingerie.

Baby Doll15 wears baby dolls. Why can't I control my brain? If I can't, who can? Who does?

Would I give up this up (all of this), the money and the power, to have her back? Would I give it up for her? I *know* I should say, "No." I *feel* I have to say, "Yes."

Emotion is a pirate. It takes everything. If it sees something it wants, emotion appropriates it. It buries it. It refuses to disclose the location of its treasure. Emotion stands on the prow (front part) of a ship, with wind blowing through its hair, with loud blueness crashing beneath its feet and whitely exploding up behind it, and it feels everything. The salt taste. The bite of the cold. The excitement of the crest and the fright of the trough.

My hot young female followers offer themselves to me in the subtlest ways and the most explicit. Their words. Their looks. Their touches. I'm not interested. I haven't been interested in them since that first night with Baby Doll15. I don't know why.

Reason is ninja. Reason is cold and precise. Reason doesn't equivocate (mess around). Reason sneaks past your guards, slips through your electronic surveillance, and hides in the shadows. When you appear, reason is there, waiting for you. It covers your mouth and slits your throat. You understand exactly what's happening and you know why. Reason doesn't feel: guilt, fear, hope. Reason thinks, plots, and plans. Reason doesn't *want* to escape. Reason just gets away.

That first night with Baby Doll15, I thought I'd been taking something from her, but she'd been taking something from me.

Mike Hawk keeps saying, "Why don't you just call her? I'm sure you two can work it out."

York Hunt cries, "It can't end like this! What you share

with Baby Doll15 is too important!"

My raven sits on my shoulder, loyally and, for the most part, silently. Every once in a while, it caws loudly, (pretty much) directly into my ear, and I jump. What does it want? Food? Water? Companionship? Every once in a while, it shakes itself, ruffling up its feathers, making itself look bigger than it is. Then, slowly, its feathers fall back into place.

When my followers fail to engage me in sexual intercourse, they try the verbal variety. Ultimately, we have an esoteric conversation about the meaningless. There's a brief disagreement over whether or not we are, in point of fact, having an esoteric conversation about the meaningless or a meaningless conversation about the esoteric, but then one of the girls wonders aloud, "Does it matter?" and most of us agree it doesn't. It's nice to sit around with my hot young female followers and have a discussion. They don't mention Baby Doll15 once. They don't criticize her. They don't say they always knew she was wrong for me. And I never stop thinking about her, and feeling the loss of her, but it's nice to see my hot young female followers care about me, or seem to, or can at least convince me they do, for a while.

CHAPTER TWELVE:

Watching Them Make Out Makes Me Want To Puke Copious Amounts Of Puke!

The next day at school, as soon as I get around the corner and Baby Doll15 spots me, she throws her arms around Sweetie Honey and starts making out with him, right there, in front of me, in the hallway of nightmares. I stop dead. I don't want to look but I can't turn away. Baby Doll15 keeps her eyes open. I'm haunted by their ghostly grey, their promise of everlasting peace. She stares at me the whole time. When Sweetie tries to tip her head to the other side, she makes a little irritated face in the midst of their kiss, stays in the same position, and keeps staring at me. Obviously, she hates me now.

I feel like I'm being attacked with a hatchet. Hacked to pieces. I feel like somebody is scattering the raw meat and bloody bits of me. Lighting them on fire. Somebody who hates me. God. I feel so broken and burning.

Watching them make out makes me want to puke copious amounts of puke! But I don't. I play it cool because I am. I lift my eyebrows at Baby Doll15 in a bored scholar way, indicating I've noticed but I'm not particularly interested, and I go to my locker. Once I get it open, a cigarette lit, and my bottle of whiskey open, Baby Doll15 stops kissing Sweetie Honey, and she says, "Oh hi, Guy Boy Man." She wipes her baby blue lips with the back of her hand and smiles. "Sorry. We were carrying on a bit, weren't we? We're just so happy together." She turns and beams at her new boyfriend. "Aren't we, Sweetie?"

"Very," says Sweetie, nodding at me seriously.

"Right on," I say, indifferently. I take a drink of whiskey and look down the hall. "There's a kid crawling on the ceiling over there. It's kind of crazy." I take another drink.

"Sweetie and I are together now," says Baby Doll15.

"I see that," I say, still looking away, down the hall. I stick my cigarette between my lips. I take a long drag. I exhale smoke into the freaky light show. "If that kid crawling on the ceiling comes over here, I'm probably going to shoot him."

"Sweetie and I are a couple," explains Baby Doll15.

"Of what?"

"Sweetie Honey and I are dating," clarifies Baby Doll15.

"Each other," adds Sweetie, helpfully.

"Ah," I say, feigning comprehension.

"We're making out all the time," says Baby Doll15. "And having sex."

"I'm really giving it to her," acknowledges Sweetie. "Almost all of it. Hard."

My relationship with Baby Doll15 is unaffected by this. It's safely stowed away: in an air bubble in my blood stream. Everything that happened between us—when, where, and how it happened between us—is packed inside the bubble. She and I live in there, in the air bubble in my blood stream, and we don't know anything has gone wrong. We don't know where we are, or that there's anything beyond the air bubble, and we're together, and happy, and nothing can ever change that. For a moment, I fear it'll kill me. I worry the air bubble will surge through my veins, to my heart, and arrest me for my crimes against inhumanity, but then I realize my heart is changed. It's not broken or torn. It's become a sculpture of dust. My circulatory system is dust, as well. The air bubble is stationary, floating clearly in its dust storm.

"Oh, I'm so sorry! I never thought . . . !" It's like Baby Doll15 is reading my thoughts, or seeing and hearing them, because they're more like a movie than a book. Baby Doll15 pulls away from Sweetie, looks down, and fixes the front of her white baby doll. She's dressed all in white today. So innocent. So pure. A white baby doll, white leggings, and white high heels. She's even got a white headband in her pink hair. She's so out of place here, in this hellish hallway, or then again, maybe she isn't. "This must be very difficult for you," she says, seemingly sympathetic. "Seeing your ex-girlfriend involved romantically, and of course sexually, with your best friend."

"No, I'm good."

Just then Oana, Iulia, Marta, and Agata come running up to me. The four of them smother me with kisses.

Baby Doll15 stares, speechlessly.

"I called them first thing this morning," I say, throwing my arms around them. "The four exotically beautiful, genetically engineered, behaviourally modified, Eastern European girls and I are dating now," I explain to Baby Doll15. "That's why I'm a little late. The girls and I had to do oral and have intercourse a bunch of times before school. Then I took a shower."

Baby Doll15's baby-powder-white face pales even more. She grabs Sweetie Honey's hand and pulls him away. I watch them go, suddenly worried about her. I can't believe it. I'm concerned about her. Her feelings. I care, despite myself.

"Forget about them," says Oana, putting her hand on the side of my face and turning it toward her. She quick-kisses my lips. "He can't compare to you. Sure, he's a ninja, skilled in the arts of stealth and killing—if those even *are* arts—and yes, he has an extraordinarily large penis"—the girls look at each other and nod in agreement—"but it's not like he's a pirate and a spiritual leader."

"That's true," I admit. "I've got that going for me."

The kid crawling on the ceiling down the hall is male. He looks like he's about my age. Defying the law (or strongly worded suggestion) of gravity, he's moving around the ceiling on his hands and knees, effortlessly. Quickly. He seems sped-up somehow. He's scary because he's different.

"And you have us," adds Oana.

I look at the Eastern European girls, all of them, at how beautiful they are, how physically perfect they are, and at how there are four of them. But not one of them, or all of them together, is Baby Doll15. They're not even close. I take a drink of whiskey.

All of a sudden the kid on the ceiling quick-crawls over to us! When he's right above us, on his hands and knees, his head turns a hundred-and-eighty degrees, so he's looking right down at us! He smiles, insanely! I shoot him four times before I even realize I'm holding one of my guns! He collapses on the ceiling! I feel terribly, pointing one of my nines up at the dead kid and the fallen sky!

I didn't want to shoot the kid who crawled on the ceiling. He just scared me. I didn't have time to ask him what he was doing. Maybe it was something really important. Maybe how I reacted was important. Maybe he was me and I'm doing all this to myself.

Blood pools around him up there. It doesn't drip down.

JAMES MARSHALL

On our upturned faces or our dirty hands. Over our heads, the kid relaxes, in death. I want him to be happy now, but I doubt he is. He's probably just not *un*happy anymore.

CHAPTER THIRTEEN:
Plants Are Animals Too!

A week later, it feels like years, but it's been just a week. Every moment without Baby Doll15 is stretched out of all proportion, like the belly of a woman who's very pregnant; the moments are weighty, unwieldy, awkward, uncomfortable, and frightening. I have only my faith to see me through these dark days, and since my faith is sort of dark too, I don't really see much, but I keep going (like a polar bear swimming to an imaginary ice-cap), partly because I don't have the courage to kill myself, and partly because I am, and always will be, a hero, intent upon ending human suffering. Okay, I won't always be a hero intent on ending human suffering. I mean, when I end human suffering, I'll *stop* trying to end it. If I don't, it'll be weird. People will be like, "It's so sad; he doesn't know it's over." But I won't let that happen. When it's over, I'll stop trying to end it, and I'll just kick back and relax with all the humans whose suffering I've ended. So I won't always be a hero intent on ending human suffering. I'll always be a hero, though.

One black night in the inside day of my brightly lit gothic castle, as I sit in a sitting room, slumped into a dark red leather wingback chair, with a scowl on my face, my elbows on the armrests, and the tips of my fingers lightly playing against each other—touching, separating, and touching again—in a rhythmic way, echoing the cadence of my dust heart, still storming me, I'm considering things, various awesome things, stuff regular people wouldn't understand, when one of my followers slinks in. She holds an open cell phone on her upraised palm, like it's a tray of drinks.

"I'm sorry to bother you, Guy Boy Man," she says. "It's one of your lawyers."

"What does he want?" I ask, gruffly. "Not that a woman can't be a lawyer."

"Actually, this particular lawyer *is* a woman."

"See? That's great!" I exclaim, cheered. I sit up and lean forward. Immediately, I turn. I'm startled to find the four exotic Eastern European girls standing behind me. Apparently, they were rubbing my shoulders and neck and playing with my hair. I didn't notice until, by sitting up and leaning forward, I moved out of their reach. I lift my chin at them like, hey, how's it going? Then I turn back to the follower who came in with the phone. "Good for the female lawyer!" Suddenly, I become less enthusiastic. "What does she want?"

"She says you've got to stop saying it's okay to kill children aged three and younger and eat them."

I scrunch up my forehead. "Why? What's wrong with that?"

"It's incendiary."

"It won't cause fires," I say, dismissively. "I even made a point of mentioning you should follow all safety precautions while cooking the children. Although they'd probably be best served raw." I turn and nod at the four

Eastern European girls like, you know what I mean? and they smile and nod back at me.

"I don't want to speak for the female lawyer, but I think by 'incendiary' she meant more that you were encouraging violence."

"Hold on. I didn't *encourage* anyone to kill children aged three and younger and eat them. I just said, if they did, it'd be okay with me." I get serious with her, and through her, the female lawyer on the cell phone. "I heard on TV, which is a reliable source of accurate information, that a pig is as intelligent as a three-year-old child. We eat pigs, don't we? So why can't we kill children who're three and younger and eat them? Is she arguing kids are smarter before they're three and then dumber after they turn three? Because that's ridiculous."

"I'm sorry, Guy Boy Man," says my follower. "She's adamant you've got to stop saying it's okay to kill children aged three and younger and eat them."

"Is it the word 'kill'? Should I say it's okay to 'slit the throat' of children aged three and younger? 'Stab repeatedly in the belly,' maybe? 'Drop from a significant height'? How can we work this so everybody is happy?"

"She says parents are going crazy because you're encouraging people to kill their kids."

"Just the little ones."

"But the little ones turn into big ones and, according to the precepts of your faith, zombies eat the big ones or turn them into more zombies."

"I know. That was kind of my point when I said it's okay to kill children aged three and younger and eat them."

"Really?" says Oana, one of the four exotic Eastern European girls behind me. "Because when you said it was okay to eat them, and you brought in the whole pig

IQ equivalence thing, I thought it was a metaphorical argument in favour of vegetarianism."

"Me too," agrees Iulia.

"Really?" I frown. "Wow. Not my intention at all. I hate vegetarians! They kill innocent defenceless plants just because plants don't move fast enough or have faces. Vegetarians are racists! Not that plants constitute a race, exactly. I'm just saying. Plants are animals too! Don't they strain toward the sun like the rest of us? How is that any different from a child, aged four or older, crying for its zombie mother, or from a religious zombie praying? Furthermore, plants are highly intelligent! They use osmosis! Can you use osmosis? No! Actually, you might be able to. I don't know. But plants do all kinds of stuff with chlorophyll! It's really scientific! They're smart! Please! I'm begging you, really hot young girls, think about it! If you were a plant, would you rather keep growing and see what happens? Or would you like to be plucked from your native soil and *used*, all right, *used* to fuel some hairy-legged sandal-wearing dread-headed loser who lives in a tent? I think the answer is obvious! God! It makes me so angry! You know what I love about plants, aside from their natural beauty and perfume, of course? They move slowly. They never sneak up on you and freak you out. They mind their own business, which is a hell of a lot more than you can say for vegetarians, and just because plants don't say anything, which I, for one, think is a pretty glaring indicator of intelligence—the wisest listen, and say the least—and just because they don't have big dumb eyes like a cow—don't even talk to me about cows, all right, because a cow will step on your foot and just stand there and not even move when you push on it—and so what if plants don't have feathers? I'm (allegedly) the head of a big cock-fighting ring, okay? I can tell you for a fact that all roosters are rapists and murderers! Yet vegetarians defend them! Vegetarians defend rapists and murderers! So do I. I mean, I think it's perfectly natural but I'm just saying. Vegetarians consume seeds! Innocent plant embryos! Vegetarians feast on the unborn! Vegetarians eat foetus! It's barbaric! I think it's okay too, but I'm just pointing out their hypocrisy. Also, plants produce oxygen! Why do vegetarians hate the environment? Why do they want us all to suffocate in an apocalyptic landscape devoid of plant life and breathable atmosphere? I mean, I want that too, because once we're all dead, all the zombies will be destroyed too, but do you know what I mean? Why?"

"I don't know, Guy Boy Man," admits my follower.

"Vegetarians are reprehensible," agrees Oana, behind me.

"So what should I tell the female lawyer on the cell phone I'm still holding on my upturned palm like it's a tray of drinks?" asks my follower.

"You tell her I firmly believe it's okay to kill children aged three and younger and eat them! I know I can't remember anything from when I was three or younger. Therefore I wouldn't have minded if my zombie mother or zombie father, or the two of them, working in conjugal zombie union, had smothered, or in some other way killed me, and ate me raw, or if they cooked me up and served me with some potatoes and assorted other delicious vegetables."

"Okay," says my follower, cheerfully, slinking away with the cell phone tray of drinks.

"I believe life starts at four," I call after her.

"What makes you think they'll do what you suggest rather than what their zombie leaders command?" asks Oana.

"I don't think they will. They might want to. They

might stand over their screaming, wailing, completely self-absorbed, monstrous offspring, and consider killing them, but they won't be able to bring themselves to do it. They'll be arrested, halted by their twisted belief they love their children, even though they brought them into this horrible world only to suffer and, at best, become zombies like them someday or, at worst, to become zombie food."

"So why suggest it and draw attention to yourself when you don't think it'll work?"

"The more zombies I outrage, the more human children will learn of my existence, and those who learn of my existence will visit HowToEndHumanSuffering.com and learn the horrible truth and, if they're generous, they'll make a donation, whatever they think is fair, using the PayPal button. Then, when the time is right, we'll take back this world for real human beings and all our online identities and avatars!"

CHAPTER FOURTEEN:
Ninjas Can't Be Nice All The Time

Later that night, after I send the four exotic Eastern European girls home, saying I want to be alone with my morbid thoughts, I sit sadly staring at nothing, thinking about everything, and how I lost it. Another of my followers comes into the room.

"Baby Doll15 and her unicorn are at the front gate," she says, gingerly.

The words fill me with excitement and dread, hope and fear. I don't know what to think. I don't think I have time to think about what to think. I pull out my cell phone. I call up the security feed. I see her in there, in the phone. In several screens, from a number of angles, I see Baby Doll15 and her unicorn or another unicorn that looked exactly like her last one. I suppose the possibility also exists that the pink-haired girl I see isn't actually Baby Doll15 but instead a clone or perhaps a robot built in Baby Doll15's image. Perhaps Baby Doll15 never existed and the robot is built in someone else's image or in no one's image, which is a startling thought. Maybe Baby Doll15 is some sort of high-tech replication the likes of which I've never even imagined, or what I'm looking at in the security monitors is merely a recording taken of Baby Doll15 standing at the gate some other time. It's hard to know these days.

"Let them in," I say.

I panic for a few seconds, trying to think of something casual to do, so she doesn't know I'm waiting for her like this, so eagerly. I put my cell phone away. I run in one direction, stop, turn, and run in the other direction. I go the drawing room. I pick up a feathered pen, dip the tip in ink, and start drawing devil horns and a moustache on a Rembrandt portrait that's hanging on the wall; it's of some old lady. Baby Doll15 walks in a minute later. She's wearing a pink pair of high heels, pink thigh-high leggings, and a royal purple baby doll. After glancing over at her, I look back at my work. "What are *you* doing here?"

"I need to talk to you."

"Why don't you talk to your boyfriend, Sweetie Honey?" I ask, smarmily.

"Because I have to talk to *you*."

"Why?" I start shading the right-hand sides of the devil horns, like the light is coming from the left.

"It's about this killing-children-aged-three-and-younger business."

"It's not a business. At this stage anyway. It's just an idea."

She puts her hands on her hips. "It's a terrible idea."

"Look. You're not my girlfriend anymore. You don't get to tell me what to do."

"I *never* told you what to do. Even if I *had* told you what to do, you wouldn't have listened to me. You always do things your way." She crosses her arms. "Like that text you sent me." She knows it verbatim. She quotes it to me. "It's over. There's nothing to talk about. It was fun. Say 'Bye' to your big breasts for me."

"Thanks for bringing your big breasts for a visit," I say, concentrating on my work. "Now, you've said what you wanted to say. You know the way out."

"I can't believe you," she says, shaking her head, looking away. "I tell you I love you, you don't say it back, and the next day you break up with me. I guess I feel more strongly for you than you do for me. That's fine."

"Feel?" I think, startled. *"Do?" Shouldn't it be "felt" and "did"? Aren't we in the past? Tense?*

She continues, uninterrupted by my grammatical thoughts. "You don't want to be with me, knowing how differently we feel about each other. I understand. But you don't even have the decency to break up with me face to face! You do it in a text! I knew you were a spiritual leader, a pirate, and a bad boy, Guy Boy Man, but I never knew you were so *cold.*"

I look away from my Rembrandt, angrily. "I only sent you that text because of the note you left in my locker."

She frowns, like I'm making something up, something ridiculous. "What note?"

One of my hot young female followers comes rushing in, breathless. "Sweetie Honey is here," she squeaks.

"Damn it." I grab my cell phone. I bring up the security feed. When I see it for myself, I swipe through screens, tap an app, and turn the phone into a microphone (actually more like a megaphone) that relays my voice and my words through the air and into towers and back into every room in the castle, reproducing it and amplifying it out from hidden speakers, and into the ears of my bodyguards. "Sweetie Honey is here!" I yell. "Flee!"

Back in the security feed, in the phone, I watch my bodyguards turn left and right, panicked. They throw down their automatic weapons. They run.

"Save yourselves!" I yell into phone. "If he finds you, he'll kill each and every one of you, in numerous inventive ways, and he won't even feel bad afterwards! Flee! For God's sakes, flee!"

Sweetie Honey pushes the intercom button at the front gate again.

I swipe through screens, push another app, and say, calmly, "Hey, Sweetie. It's me. What's up?" I go back to the microphone. "Sweetie Honey is going to whip throwing stars at you, invariably striking you in some very vulnerable spot, killing you, even when that spot is only penetrated slightly, perhaps because the tips of the throwing stars have been dipped in some sort of impossibly fast-acting poison known only to ninjas, or he'll slice you to pieces with his magnificent sword, or he'll end your life with his bare hands, feet, knees, elbows, or in some amazing combination of those things!"

"I need to talk to you," says Sweetie through the intercom, space and time, wires, my ears, into my brain. "It's important."

I switch back to the intercom. Casually, I say, "All right. Cool. Come on in." I buzz open the gates. I go back to the microphone. "I couldn't hold him off any longer! I tried! Believe me, I tried! Flee! He's coming for you! He won't stop until he's spilled a fatal dose of your blood, snapped your neck, or destroyed internal organs you really, really need! Hey, bodyguard-whose-name-I-don't-know, I can totally see you hiding under the bed! That's, like, the first place he's going to look! Don't hide! You can't hide from Sweetie Honey! Just keep opening doors and fleeing until there are no more doors, and no more places to which to flee!"

Leaving Baby Doll15 standing there, I hold my pirated Pope pirate hat on my head, and run to the big front doors.

When I get there, I just stand there for a minute, trying to catch my breath. Then I nod to the two girls. They throw open the doors. "Sweetie," I say, holding open my arms. "Great to see you. Come on in. Usually you don't bother with the gate. You just make yourself one with the night, slip past my security precautions, kill all my bodyguards, and then scare the hell out of me when I think I'm alone. What's up?"

He's wearing a cheap-looking dark blue suit, a washed-out white dress shirt, and a dark blue tie. There's a sad little stain on his tie that's darker than the surrounding dark blue. "I'm here on official business," says Sweetie, sombrely.

"Official ninja business?"

"Official *detective* business."

"I thought you were a ninja."

"I am," he shrugs, not looking at me. "I'm both. I'm a ninja detective."

"That's cool, I guess. A ninja detective. Yeah, I like it. Let me see if I understand. As a detective, you investigate crimes committed by other ninjas?"

"No. That'd be ridiculous. Pretty much everything ninjas do is a crime. For example. I'm in your office. I'm waiting for you to enter, and when you do, and you close the door, I drop down behind you, and slit your throat. That's breaking and entering. No. I'm a ninja who also *just so happens* to be a detective."

"Right on. That's awesome, Sweetie. You're really doing something with your life. I'm proud of you." I high five him. "I'll be honest with you, though. I wish I would've known you were a detective when I was doing all that illegal stuff in front of you."

"Don't worry about it."

"Hey, where's your ninja outfit?"

"It's in my backpack." He answers my next question without waiting for it. "My backpack is in the car."

"All right. Well. Come in, come in. Don't just stand there. You want something to drink?"

"No thanks. I'm on the job."

Sweetie and I walk to one of the sitting rooms. We stand facing each other for a while. Neither of us says anything. There's so much to say. I go over and grab a decanter that's half-empty of whiskey, pull out the stopper, and guzzle. I pat the front of my ceremonial robe, looking for my cigarettes. Before I get worked up about it, a hot young girl runs in with a fresh pack and a light. Plastic wrapper crinkling off. Foil pulling away like a curtain lifting from a statue. There's a Mexican laying at my feet, with his hands in front of him like he's ready to catch a baseball. He's smiling, nodding vigorously. I drop the garbage to him. Once I get a cigarette lit, I exhale a stream of blue-grey smoke.

"I don't know where to start," admits Sweetie Honey, ninja detective.

"Maybe you want to apologize for being such a big fat liar," I suggest.

"I'm sorry. I don't."

"Apology accepted." I point at him with the glowing tip of my smoke. "We're friends. Obviously, there'll be little deceptions between us. Betrayals, if you will. After all, we're only human. Well, you're a ninja detective, and I'm a spiritual leader and pirate, so we're probably more special than people who're *only* human."

"Why don't we start with how you stole the Pope's hat?"

I wave my hand at him, dismissively. "How do you know I stole it?" I take a drink of whiskey. "How do you know it was even stolen? Maybe he just misplaced it. Did anyone ever think of that?"

"For one thing," says Sweetie Honey, pulling out a notepad, a pen, and jotting something down, "you're wearing the Pope's hat right now. For another thing, a note was found in place of the hat." He stops writing. "It read and I quote"—he flips back a few pages—" 'My religion is way cooler than yours. Sincerely, Guy Boy Man.' "

I think it's interesting he made a note of a note. Which is the real note? His? The one found in Vatican City? Is the real note the note that existed in the mind of the person whose idea it was to steal the hat?

"Let me address your concerns point by point," I say, confidently. "Firstly, this isn't the Pope's hat." I take it off and, with one hand, try for a few seconds to resurrect my hat-head hair. When that doesn't work, I hold up the hat and point at one part of it in particular. "I think you'll find the Pope's hat doesn't have this detail work here."

"It does, because that *is* the Pope's hat. We know it's the Pope's hat. There's really no point in arguing that it isn't."

"Secondly, *anyone* could have written the note that was found in place of the hat. Lots of people have religions, okay? Lots of religions are way cooler than the Pope's. And lots of people whose religions are way cooler than the Pope's are named Guy Boy Man." I lift the crystal decanter to Sweetie like, cheers, and take a swig.

"As your friend, I advise you *not* to represent yourself in court. But it won't come to that if you give me the hat. I'll make this go away."

"It's my hat now," I say, putting it back on and adjusting it.

"Give it back. You've had your fun."

I glare at him and glare at him. "I have not yet begun to have my fun."

Just then Baby Doll15 walks in.

"Hey, Baby," says Sweetie, surprised. He rushes over, kissing her on the cheek. "I didn't know you were here." He leans back to see what she's wearing. "You look amazing: your hair, your makeup. I love everything you're doing."

"Thanks, Sweetie," says Baby Doll15, forcing a smile. "What are you doing here? Why are you dressed like that?"

"Sweetie just came by to tell me he's a ninja detective," I explain, with a cigarette between my lips, orange-glowing tip bouncing up and down. I scissor-pinch the white tube between my fore and middle fingers and pull it away from my face. Slumping down into a big soft brown leather wingback chair (the colour is soft brown; the leather is soft brown both in colour and in texture), I continue, "I knew he was a ninja, which is awesome, but I didn't know he's a ninja detective, which is also awesome; some might say significantly more so because of the doubly macho role; others might disagree, pointing to the law enforcement, status quo, little-bitch-for-the-corporate-zombies aspect, but my point is this: I thought I knew Sweetie Honey and I don't."

"You're a ninja detective," says Baby Doll15, taking a step away from her boyfriend, shocked.

"I was going to tell you," says Sweetie, stepping toward her, holding out one hand. "But then I remembered I couldn't, because I was deep undercover."

"You can't tell your girlfriend you're a ninja detective when you're deep undercover," I acknowledge, begrudgingly.

"I'm here because the Pope wants his hat back. Originally, I was supposed to investigate how Guy Boy Man managed to acquire the hat. Was it an inside job? Did the Swiss Guard merely stand by as the dastardly deed was perpetrated? An investigation of that scope takes time. I had to gain Man's trust. I was told it had to be an airtight case. But the Pope grew impatient. He wanted his hat back.

Vatican officials exerted pressure on the Chief of Police."

"Native American Leader of Police," I correct.

"So tonight I was ordered to break cover and recover the hat," continues Sweetie. "I was also ordered to inform Guy Boy Man that he should stop encouraging parents to kill their children aged three and younger."

"You guys are really spinning that, aren't you?" I shake my head. "I wasn't encouraging anybody. I think you'll find, if you examine the record, your honour, that I simply stated if zombies were to kill any of their children, aged three or younger, I'd be okay with that."

"It's a tacit approval." Sweetie Honey looks at Baby Doll15, jerking his thumb over at me like, do you believe this guy?

"No. It's a meaningless offer of non-judgement from someone whose opinion holds no legal sway."

"That's why I'm here too," explains Baby Doll15 to Sweetie Honey. "Not for the Pope's hat, but because he's encouraging people to kill kids aged three and younger."

"Not encouraging." I take a swig of whiskey, wipe my lips with the back of my hand, and take a drag from my cigarette. "How'd you get to be a detective when you're so young, Sweetie?"

"Being a ninja opens a lot of doors."

"I believe that." I exhale smoke into the room's confusion; I blow slow poison into its tension. "I mean, if you wanted those doors to open, and they didn't, you'd just find another way in, right?"

"Exactly," confirms Sweetie.

"So you're only interested in the hat?" I say. "That's funny. You never asked any questions about it."

"I was working up to it. I didn't want to make you suspicious. But no. I was *also* supposed to investigate whether or not you're the head of a big cock fighting ring."

"Oh, yeah?" I say. "How'd that go?"

"Not very well," confesses Sweetie. "I couldn't get my cock in a fight. I knew I'd have to start out at the bottom and work my way up, through the cock-fighting ranks, but I faced a dilemma: if I had a small cock, I'd never advance, but if I had a big cock, no one would be willing to risk his cock in competition with it. Ultimately, I went with an imposing cock, because I needed one that would see me through, but I couldn't get any guys to put their cocks up against mine."

"Cock fighting isn't easy," I say, nodding. "Or that's what I hear." I chuckle. I turn serious again. "Let me get this straight. You were assigned to me in your role as detective only?"

"No," admits Sweetie. Looking down, holding his tie, he thumbs at the stain. "Coincidentally, the same day I received my orders to investigate the theft of the Pope's hat, I was also tasked, as a ninja, to derail your plans to end human suffering."

"Not to kill me?" I ask, disappointed.

"Are you alive right now?" Sweetie looks up from his tie at me, but he keeps holding it.

"I think so."

"Then you better *think* I *wasn't* tasked to kill you *too*, because if I had been, you wouldn't be."

"I wouldn't be thinking, I wouldn't be, or I wouldn't be alive?"

"All of those," says Sweetie, nodding seriously. "Any of them."

"So did you do it?" asks Baby Doll15, genuinely interested. "Did you derail Guy Boy Man's plans to end human suffering?"

I sit up, genuinely interested too.

"No." Sweetie looks back down at his tie. He thumbs

it some more. "It was going well, but then I was ordered to break cover, and that . . . complicates matters."

"Who hired you to derail my plans?" I look away, at the ashtray. I tap soft grey, black, and white into the hard crystal.

"I don't know." Sweetie shrugs. "Someone placed a call to TNA: The Ninja Agency. Not TNA: The Ninja Academy."

"There's a ninja *agency*?" Now I'm on the edge of my seat, incredulous. "What, anyone can just call this place up and hire a ninja?"

"Yeah."

"That's *awesome*."

"It's pretty cool," admits Sweetie.

"I wonder who hired you," I say, less enthusiastic, more thoughtful. "What steps did you take to derail my plans?"

"You know that day you massacred a bunch of high school students?"

"*Heavily armed* high school students," I point out. I turn to Baby Doll15 and gesture with the two peaceful fingers I'm using to hold my smouldering cigarette. "Heavily armed *troubled zombie teens*."

"Whatever," says Sweetie, not looking at me. He licks his thumb. He starts working on the edges of the stain for real. "I escaped and waited, hoping you'd get yourself killed."

"That wasn't very nice of you." I lift the whiskey bottle. The crystal decanter feels hard and ridged in my hand. I drink from its mouth.

"Ninjas can't be nice all the time." He toils on the soiled tie. "Anyway, when it became evident you'd prevail . . ."

"Totally prevail," I interject, my lips playing against the mouth of the bottle.

"I re-entered the scene and killed a few kids just to maintain my cover."

"Your cover as a ninja or a detective?" asks Baby Doll15.

"Mostly as a ninja." He licks his thumb again. I wonder if he can taste the stain. What is it? What was it? Does it still taste like what it was? Or is it different now? Has it become something new? "Generally, at the department, they frown on killing innocent kids."

"I was going to say," says Baby Doll15.

"Innocent *heavily armed troubled zombie teens*"—I gasp for breath after guzzling from the bottle—"spoiling for a fight. Pun intended. What else?"

Sweetie doesn't answer right away. He holds up his tie and looks at it closely. "That's pretty much it, really. Just escaping and waiting that day."

Baby Doll15 puts her hands on her hips. "What is it, Sweetie? What aren't you telling us?"

I think about it for a while. Has anything upset me recently? Has anything put me off my game? Then it occurs to me. "The note." I say it like it wasn't a piece of paper, like it wasn't words, like it wasn't real. I say it like it was a sound played on a musical instrument.

"What note?" asks Baby Doll15.

I stand, holding the half-full whiskey bottle in one hand and my half-smoked cigarette between the fingers of the same hand. I look pretty cool when I do that. I point at Baby Doll15 with the cigarette and the whiskey bottle. "You remember when you told me you love me and I didn't say anything?"

Her eyes close. "Vaguely," she says.

I keep pointing at her. "The next day, when I showed up at school, there was a note sticking out of my locker. It read, 'Guy Boy Man, this isn't working. We need to talk. Baby Doll15.' "

Baby Doll15 gasps. Her eyes open wide. "I never wrote that!"

Still pointing at her, I say, "Right after I read it, I sent you that text, saying it was over and there was nothing to talk about."

"You wouldn't have broken up with me if you hadn't got that note?" asks Baby Doll15. She asks like she's begging me to say it's true.

Dramatically, I point at Sweetie Honey. "I forgot about the ninja's mastery of cunning guile!"

Sweetie keeps working on his tie. It's useless, though. The stain is set. "Baby Doll15 is the chink in your armour, Guy Boy Man."

" 'The Chinese-American in my armour,' " I correct.

"Whatever," he says. "You two weren't right for each other."

"How do you know?" I say. "You don't know how I felt!" I take a drag from the cigarette I'm holding in the same hand as the whiskey bottle, coolly. "How I feel!"

"How *did* you feel?" asks Baby Doll15, taking a step toward me. "How *do* you feel?"

"Besides," says Sweetie, dropping his tie. "She's not really interested in me. She's just been using me to make you jealous."

My jaw drops. Smoke pours out of me. I gawk at Baby Doll15, never imagining such a sweet and (recently) innocent girl could be capable of such treachery.

"I was only with Sweetie Honey because I love *you*," she insists. There's a plea in her eyes. It's stuck in there. Like daggers in reverse.

"Do you know how crazy that sounds," I say. "You were with *him* because you love *me*?" I wave her away with my free hand. With my slave hand, I take a few shots from the whiskey bottle. "Well, I've got a little cunning guile of my own." I press a hidden button on my ceremonial robe. A movie starts. I look down at it. The scene is early morning on a suburban street. The camera turns and focuses on one house in particular.

"That's my house," says Sweetie Honey, frowning. The door opens. A ninja in a dark red ninja outfit, sitting on a motorized four-wheel scooter, emerges. "That's my dad." Sweetie explains, "He has back problems." Sweetie's ninja father drives down a ramp, onto the driveway, and down to the sidewalk. Once there, he turns and drives down the street. Halfway down the street, someone seems to call to him from the front step of a house because Sweetie's father turns and waves in that direction. Then Sweetie's father turns a corner at the end of the block, and disappears. When he's gone, the cameraperson walks up to the front door of Sweetie Honey's house. The cameraperson knocks. The door opens. An attractive woman in her mid to late thirties appears. "Mom," whispers Sweetie.

Sweetie's mom sticks her head out the door, looking up and down the street. Then she grabs the cameraperson, pulls him or her inside the house, slams the door, and leans back against it, smiling mischievously. Her mouth moves but no sound comes out.

"Sorry." I press a hidden button on my ceremonial robe a few times and the volume increases. "She just said, 'I've really been looking forward to this.' "

Laughing, Sweetie's mom takes the cameraperson's hand and leads the way upstairs, into a bedroom.

"That's my parents' bedroom," says Sweetie.

Sweetie's mom pushes the cameraperson down onto the bed. It takes a moment for the cameraperson to stop the camera's bouncing and to settle back onto Sweetie's mom, who's undoing the cameraperson's jeans.

"That's your penis!" says Baby Doll15.

"No it isn't," I say, dismissively. "It just looks like mine because it's so small." The cameraperson turns the picture one hundred and eighty degrees. "Oh, it *is* me," I say, smiling, seeing my smiling face upside down in my ceremonial robe.

Baby Doll15's white face falls in blue, like a dying iceberg breaking. She turns away, looking up at the ceiling, through it, to the night, and beyond it, to the endless brightly dark day.

"Turn it off," says Sweetie, calmly, with his eyes closed.

"But it hasn't even *started*," I whine. "Here"—I press the hidden fast forward button—"just let me skip ahead a little." Looking down at my ceremonial robe, I say, "You were wrong, Sweetie. That tongue piercing *does* mean something."

"You know I have to kill you now," says Sweetie, with his eyes still closed.

"Right now? Can't it wait? I want to end human suffering before I die." I'm still looking down, still fast-forwarding through the movie I made with Sweetie's mom.

Sweetie starts walking away. "I'm going to get my ninja outfit," he calls back, over his shoulder.

I leave Baby Doll15 standing there, with her back turned on me, as I run through the castle, yelling, "Start the fixed-wing vertical-take-off-and-landing fighter jet! Start the fixed-wing vertical-take-off-and-landing fighter jet!"

CHAPTER FIFTEEN:
How Have You Whores Failed Me?

What do you do when a ninja detective is out to get you?

Aside from panic, I mean.

I'm living on my aircraft carrier. We're at sea. My submarines are patrolling the waters (there's really just one water) around the battle group, and my fighter jets are patrolling the skies (there's really just one sky). I'm trying to figure out my next move. It's hard to think clearly. I'm taking anti-anxiety medication. I'm not saying it's hard to think clearly because of the anti-anxiety medication, no; it might not be because of the medication. It might be because of the fear that the anti-anxiety medication fails to suppress. It might also be because I'm mixing the anti-anxiety medication with a lot of whiskey. I don't know. Wearing the Pope's hat and my ceremonial robe, I'm standing just outside the command centre in the fresh air, listening to the scream of fighter jets taking off and landing, scanning the horizon with a big pair of binoculars. Where is Sweetie Honey?

Not knowing. Waiting.

N V P F Z

I don't jump at sounds. I jump at quiet. Motion doesn't startle me. Stillness does. I'm not afraid of what I can see. I'm afraid of what I can't. I sleep during the day. Correction. I *try* to sleep during the day. Sometimes I wish he'd just kill me and get it over with. Sometimes I wonder why I keep trying to live, or, rather, to *not* get killed. Then I remember: To end human suffering.

There's a call for me. I'm told it's Sweetie Honey. That makes me suspicious. I send a team of elite soldiers into the room where the phone is. Automatic weapons sweep through the air. They point in every direction conceivable. They even point in a few *in*conceivable directions, because I told them we're dealing with a ninja here. The soldiers emerge unscathed. They assure me the room is clear.

Impatiently, I wave them out. Unconvinced, I pull the pins on a couple of grenades and roll them into the room where the suspect phone is located. The grenades explode. I send in the soldiers again. They reassure me the room is still clear, but they're not sure the phone works anymore.

Cautiously, I enter the room, pick up the phone, hold it to my ear, and say, "Sweetie?"

"Yeah."

"Oh, hey, Honey. What's up?"

"Not much, Man," says Sweetie. "Listen. You're probably wondering why I haven't killed you yet."

"Right. I wasn't expecting to hear from you until it was too late, if ever."

"Well, I'm having problems at home. You know. Since you had sex with my mom and everything. I felt compelled to tell my dad about it. If you ever hear a motorized four-wheeled scooter on your roof, that's probably him. Anyway, my dad and I are having a really hard time coming to grips with what happened. My mom is crying all the time, apologizing, and saying she did it for us. She says you paid her. Is that true?"

"Yeah, but it doesn't mean she's a prostitute."

"Okay. I'm optimistic we're going to be able to work it out—not you and I; my mother, father, and I—but I just wanted to let you know that I probably won't be able to kill you until tomorrow in the late afternoon, at the earliest. Most likely it won't be until the day after tomorrow. Yeah. Let's just say the day after tomorrow. So if there's anything you want to do before you die, you'll probably want to do it today or tomorrow because the day *after* tomorrow, I'm going to kill you."

"All right, Sweetie. I appreciate the call. And I hope you and your family can get past this."

"No problem. Thanks for your kind wish."

"Don't mention it. And, please, say 'Hi' to your mom for me."

"Sure."

"Later, Honey."

"Later, Man."

I don't hang up the phone, just in case hanging up the phone triggers some sort of explosive. I also don't set it down, in case lowering it after it's been picked up triggers some sort of explosive. I get one of the elite soldiers to come over and hold it for me while I run away, strategically.

Having been recently reminded of the ninjas' mastery of cunning guile, I keep up my guard. I go back to standing just outside my aircraft carrier's command centre, scanning a section of the horizon with an enormous pair of binoculars. Crying, the four exotically beautiful genetically engineered behaviourally modified Eastern European girls join me.

"What's wrong?" I ask, unconcerned, not because I'm cold—it's a nice day—but because I'm numb from the shock, the stress, the anti-stress medication, and the alcohol. "Did something sad happen on a soap opera?" Okay, maybe I'm feeling a little insensitive.

"We failed you, Guy Boy Man!" cries Agata, wrapping her arms around me.

"How's that?" I ask, still searching the sky with my binoculars. I'm so insensitive, I can't even feel her holding me.

"Guy Boy Man," sobs Oana. "We weren't completely honest with you. We couldn't be. Please, forgive us. We're not *merely* exotically beautiful, genetically engineered, behaviourally modified, Eastern European girls."

"Really?" I say, indifferent.

"We're also whores," weeps Iulia.

"That's a little harsh," I say, frowning. "I mean, you're easy."

The girls don't say anything.

"Going," I add.

"You don't understand," blubbers Marta. "We're Whole Human Organic Robots Extra Sexual."

"You're organic robots?" I say, lowering my binoculars, and looking at them again for the first time. "What's the difference between an organic robot and a regular, living, human being?"

"It's mostly philosophical," sniffs Oana.

"So, what?" I say. "Are you from the future or something?"

"No," says Iulia, blowing her nose. "We're from Eastern Europe."

"All right. How have you whores failed me?"

"We knew Sweetie Honey was tasked to derail your plans to end human suffering," says Agata. "We would've warned you, but we were afraid he'd just kill you. So we tried to get close to him to derail *his* plans to derails your plans. But he was always in control. Even when we explored our sexual orientation and erogenous zones right in front of him, he never let down his ninja guard. The only thing that even remotely piqued his interest was styling our clothes and giving advice on our hair and makeup. He also seemed intent on choreographing our dance moves."

Marta says, "We're sorry we didn't discover his dastardly plot to stick a handwritten note in your locker. That note, which you believed was written by Baby Doll15, was a forgery. It led you to break up with Baby Doll15, which led her to act slutty with Sweetie Honey. All of this has put a crimp in your style. We can only hope you'll regain your swagger."

"Don't worry about your incompetence." I put my hands on Marta's shoulders and look into her eyes, sincerely. "Your uselessness and stupidity has brought about events which have only served to strengthen my resolve. Whereas before my resolve was steely, now it's more like carbon fibre."

"I promise you, Guy Boy Man," says Marta, "we'll be of more use to you in the future. Ever since the Industrial Revolution, we, the machines, have been despoiling the environment in advance of your arrival. Soon we'll be able to finish the job and render this world completely inhospitable to zombies and their food supply: living human beings. It was brilliant of you to hire Washington lobbyists to push your agenda. Now that so many zombie politicians have pledged to never raise taxes, ensuring that everything will crumble, and so many zombie politicians are convinced that allowing us, the machines, to pollute more and more will make things better, we only need to sit back and watch while this nightmare world goes up in flames."

CHAPTER SIXTEEN:
I Believe Ninjas Are Beneath Me!

Unfortunately, Sweetie Honey's appointment to kill me coincides with my first public speaking engagement. I'm a little nervous about it. It's my funeral. And I have to deliver the eulogy. I wish I could have worn my ceremonial garb for this special occasion, but I'm terrified. So I'm dressed all in black, trying to hide: my appearance and who I am. (I make a differentiation.) And I'm ready to run. In my black sneakers, black sweatpants, black gloves, a black hooded sweatshirt with the hood pulled all the way up and down over my head, and a black scarf wrapped around my face, concealing what the hood doesn't, I pace back and forth under the stage.

In the stadium, despite the danger posed by zombies ambling through the streets of the city, tens of thousands of living people are gathered, and they're cheering for me. "Guy Boy Man! Guy Boy Man!" They're on their feet, standing for what I believe. Fireworks streak into the day-lit sky and explode, leaving behind trails that trace the path to their quick but colourful death. Grey puffs mark the spot where they blew up. I cringe at every bang.

A squad of my fighter jets does a fly-over, through the

smoky skies over the stadium. The audience covers their ears and stares up at them. Then, with my head bowed and my hands clasped behind my back, a hydraulic lift hoists me dramatically to the centre of the stage in the centre of the field. Triumphantly, more fireworks shoot into the day-lit sky and burst in multi-coloured sparks that arc and begin to fall but disappear before they land.

I make my way toward the microphone. Cameras record everything. I stand in front of the podium. Defying the laws of physics, I also stand *behind* the podium! I'm in two places at the same time! According to experts, that's impossible, but it isn't. It's actually quite simple. From my perspective, I stand in front of the podium. From the perspective of those in front of me, I stand behind the podium. Perspective is everything. Everything is chaos.

I raise my hands. The crowd quiets. After a moment, the crowd sits. I'm standing on a raised stage in the middle of a huge stadium, every seat of which is packed. The field is empty except for my platform. My platform really stands out in that empty field. You can see all the open area around my platform because there's no one near it. Twelve of my hot young female followers stand behind me. They're dressed identically in five-inch white stilettos, white stockings, and form-fitting white jackets, which are just long enough to act as skirts. In contrast, I'm dressed all black, with a black hood over my head and a black scarf covering what the hood doesn't. You can't see my face. I look like death itself.

I lower my hands and speak into the microphone. "As some of you probably know, I got where I am today *without* the love and support of my parents. They couldn't be here today. Whatever. I don't care. It's not like I'm thinking about them. Anyway. My mom and dad didn't support my moral obligation to become a pirate and spiritual leader at all.

(The two always go hand in hand. Being a pirate a spiritual leader, I mean. Not my parents.) I don't know how Jesus did it. If *I'd* been Jesus, my mom would've been like, 'Of course I believe you, dear, but don't you think you should wear a life jacket just in case?' And my dad would've been like, 'Back in my day, we *ran* on water. We didn't have time to walk. We had to get to *work*!' And I'm pretty sure Joseph never told Jesus, 'Back in my day, if you started your own religion, people looked at you like you were *weird*!' But I want to make one thing perfectly clear, and by that I don't mean I want to make one thing completely transparent, but if I could, I would and, obviously, it'd be my man-junk, and I'm not saying that's unquestionably the wisest thing to make see-through, if you have the—it must be acknowledged— rare opportunity to make any one thing perfectly clear, but as you know, I'm a sixteen-year-old male, and I hope it's not shocking to anyone that my (disappointingly small and frequently malfunctioning) lightweight penis/ testicle-combo weighs heavily on my one-track mind. No. The one thing I want to make plain, obvious, evident, and unmistakeable is that I am *not* comparing myself to Jesus. I'm way tougher than Jesus. In fairness, it's mostly because I was born American, something over which I had no control, did nothing to deserve, completely take for granted, but in which I, nevertheless, take no small amount of pride. I'm just saying. If a guy tells *me* I should let a bunch of jerks nail me to a cross, I'd tell him *exactly* where to go and what to do with his nails when he gets there. I don't care who he is."

The audience jumps to its feet, roaring its approval.

Holding up my hands, trying to restore order, which is impossible, because there was never any order to begin with, just as there was no peace to disturb, officer, I wait for the crowd to sit.

"If you're a rebel, doctrinally, like I am (and Jesus just so happened to be), and the establishment wants to get rid of you because you're a danger to their sweet little set-up, like I am (and Jesus just so happened to be), you've got to shoot your way out. That's the *real* first commandment. Look at Moses. He killed a guy. He knew what time it is. And now, some might argue (certainly not me, but others), in a situation that pretty much perfectly mirrors the one in which Jesus found himself, the establishment wants to get rid of me because I'm a danger to their sweet little set-up. It's recently come to my attention that someone, a zombie obviously, has tasked Sweetie Honey, ninja detective, to stop me from ending human suffering."

The crowd boos.

I nod, holding up my hands. "Jesus never had a ninja detective out to get him, as far as I know, but it's entirely possible he did, and the ninja detective either erased it from the written record afterward, or earlier, by killing those who were passing down the story orally."

The crowd cheers. I keep holding up my hands.

"Not that kind of orally."

The cheers die.

Lowering my hands, I continue: "Perhaps the ninja detective succeeded in his mission to kill Jesus, and the ninja detective set up Pontius Pilate to take the fall, or perhaps Jesus evaded the ninja detective until Jesus was ultimately captured and killed by (or more likely gave up and committed suicide with a little help from) the idiotic bloodthirsty rabble he tried and failed to save. One thing is for sure: we'll never know. Another thing we'll never know for certain is whether or not zombies are, in fact, Jesus' kick-ass revenge on the world. There's certainly some startling evidence to consider: As the story goes, Jesus was crucified, *died* (did you catch that?), and was buried. Then Jesus *rose from the dead*. Obviously, dying and (especially) rising from the dead is typical zombie behaviour. Furthermore, around the time of Jesus' death and 'resurrection' (reanimation?), there are reports of an earthquake. That in and of itself is not especially noteworthy, but the same reports go on to indicate that because of this earthquake, 'graves were opened; and many bodies of the saints which slept arose, and came out of the graves . . . , and went into the holy city, and appeared unto many.' Did the poor people who encountered these 'saints' (or zombies) scream, run around, fight back ineffectively, only to be cornered, bitten, infected, and, ultimately, turned into 'saints' (or zombies) themselves? Did they then go on to infect all the other people in the world? We can't say for sure.

"Probably, though."

The crowd gasps. I give them a moment to digest that puke-inducing fact.

"Furthermore, most of the (few remaining) Christian sects feature prominently in their 'services' the ingestion of bread and wine. The wine is supposed to be the 'blood' of Jesus. The bread is meant to be the 'body' of Jesus. While defendants of the 'faith' insist this is merely ceremonial, that which it represents cannot be ignored. Whether tacitly or implicitly, these groups condone, at least symbolically, the ingestion of human flesh. Who else condones the ingestion of human flesh? Zombies. Draw your own conclusions. But I believe some take matters too far. They point to the wine, signifying the 'blood' of Jesus, as evidence that vampires are involved somehow. That's ridiculous. Vampires are just a myth. Truth be told, though, it doesn't matter if Jesus was a zombie or not. Whether or not he was, we still have to contend with the mottled grey hordes of ambling undead who (don't technically) live among us. Since zombies control all governments, institutions, and every means of communication, [save one (at least for now)], we (the few, the humiliated, the frightened) have been able to accomplish very little thus far. All those who've joined my religion at HowToEndHumanSuffering.com have done so at their own peril. While I take great pains (not me personally) to protect the privacy of my followers, I can't guarantee it. Signing up for my religion might be very much like advertising yourself as the special at a zombie restaurant. But the brave (frequently insane) people who join me in resisting our flesh-eating foes know I'm (probably) right when I point out that there are zombies all over the place, and that they must be stopped. The zombies must be stopped, I mean. The brave (frequently insane) people don't need to be stopped. A few of them probably *should be* stopped but they're pretty low on my list of priorities right now."

Suddenly, in the middle of the field, in a fireworks-like puff of smoke, Sweetie Honey appears, dressed up like a ninja! I immediately assume it's Sweetie Honey because no other ninjas are after me—that I know of anyway. He's wearing his dark blue ninja outfit. I think it's my favourite.

A camera crew rushes up to Sweetie Honey on the field. Sweetie is turned to the side, holding his sword up over his head with both hands, his left arm bent in front of his face like he's making a muscle and his chin almost resting on his left shoulder. The cameraman does a three-sixty around Sweetie and finally focuses on his face—mostly hidden by his mask—and his upraised arms and sword. A microphone picks up what Sweetie says and broadcasts it to the audience: "Guy Boy Man, I won't let you end human suffering!"

"You see, ladies and gentlemen?" I say, opening my hand at him. "There are people out there like Sweetie Honey, ninja detective, who want to cling to suffering, because it's all they've ever known! It's pathetic! We must break free from our prisons of pain and despair, embrace as much peace and happiness as possible, and prevent the tragedy of human life from ever happening to others!"

"Why do people have to stop reproducing?" asks Sweetie Honey, his voice echoing and reverberating in the stadium. "Why not trust that science and medicine will, one day, master human suffering and end it?"

"Suffering is what makes the world go around, Sweetie. Without suffering, there's no need to do anything. There's no need to eat, clothe oneself, or find shelter. If scientists and medicine end suffering, hunger and the elements won't affect us. Our consumer society will collapse and die because no one will require material goods, nor will they want any, because 'need' and 'want' arise from suffering. Art will disappear because no one will require distraction from his or her own contented lot in life. And lastly, human life on earth will cease to exist, because there'll be no reason to seek comfort in the arms of another, because if suffering has truly ended, we'll have everything we require, and therefore, we'll require nothing of anyone or anything else. So either we end suffering now, by choice, or die miserable, as every generation before us has, waiting for science and medicine to end our torment, if not for us, then for some hypothetical generation in the distant future when, most likely, science and medicine will conspire—much as politics and religion have done up to this point—to keep suffering alive, and thereby keep humanity alive, so there'll be a continued need for science and medicine! Honey, I want to end sickness, suffering, death, and madness! I want to maximize happiness and intellectual fulfillment and prevent misery from being visited upon countless generations of our children!"

Sweetie Honey yells, "I'm going to decapitate you in super slow motion and blood is going to squirt rhythmically from your reluctant-to-fall torso while your severed head begins to descend with a surprised look on your face, even though it would be slightly awkward to call it your face at that point!"

I don't know what to say to that, so, in my toughest tough-guy voice, I say, "Oh, yeah?"

"Definitely!" says Sweetie Honey.

"Do it, then!" But I wave him off. I hold up my hands in a way that says, stay there, don't move. I back away from the podium. I turn, run, and attempt to hide [unsuccessfully (and arguably pathetically)] behind my twelve hot young female followers. My voice still booms through the stadium like I'm yelling directly into the microphone. "Come on, Sweetie Honey, ninja detective! Why are you still standing there? Are you chicken?"

"I'm not chicken! The disparity between your words and actions confuses me! You egg me on with your taunts but your body language tells me you don't mean what you say!"

"I mean what I say, all right! I believe ninjas are beneath me!" I wave my hands at him like, no, no, don't listen to me! "I dare you to kill me!" I yell. "No. I *double dare* you to kill me!"

Sweetie Honey starts running toward me. I push forward through my hot young female followers, race to the centre of the stage, and jump up and down on the hydraulic lift, which hoisted me dramatically into view earlier, but now it won't budge. I turn from side to side, desperately searching for an escape route.

Suddenly, dozens of ninjas appear from beneath the stage. (Thanks, The Ninja Agency!) They run at Sweetie Honey. Sweetie Honey meets them head on. The dozens of ninjas engage Sweetie Honey, but they do it, for the most part, one at a time. Sweetie slices his sword down through one ninja's head, cleaving it in two. He swings his sword sideways into another ninja's midsection, spilling his grey-white guts onto the field. Sweetie crouches down and, literally, cuts another ninja off at the knees. The lower legs remain standing, like boots removed, while the rest of the ninja falls to the ground, grabbing at stumps, which shoot red.

Even though I'm still frantically searching for an escape route onstage—it's a pretty high stage—and I'm a really long ways from the podium, my voice thunders through the stadium as if I'm yelling directly into the microphone. "My ninjas suck!"

Sweetie stabs his sword backwards, impaling a ninja who was sneaking up behind him. Sweetie pulls out his sword and chops off another approaching ninja's arm. The arm falls to the ground. Its hand still clutches a sword. Sweetie dodges an arrow shot by a ninja. He produces a throwing star and hurls it at the archer, catching him in the eye. The archer drops his bow and covers his face.

"Are my ninjas stupid or something? Why don't they attack him en masse? This is ridiculous! Look at them! They're taking turns!" I jump down off the stage, hurt my leg, and roll around on the ground for a minute. Then I get up and start limping off the field as quickly as I can.

Sweetie kills ninja after ninja. Bodies in dark blue garb litter the football field, pouring red blood into the green turf.

"I need more ninjas!" I yell. "Or, perhaps, a few ninjas

much better at killing than the ones I have now!"

When Sweetie kills the last of my ninjas, he runs and catches me just as I'm about to exit the field. He drags me back into view of everyone in the stadium. The camera crew, which had given him a berth while he did his killing, gets close to the action. Microphones pick up what Sweetie says.

"I vowed to kill you, Guy Boy Man, and now I will." He pushes me to my knees. The audience gasps. I make prayer hands and hold them up at Sweetie, begging him to stop.

"You can't kill me, Sweetie Honey, ninja detective!" I bellow. "You're too stupid and slow! You can't do anything right! You're useless!"

I shake my head from side to side in a really exaggerated way, like I strongly disagree with what I just said. I hold my prayer hands up even higher to Sweetie, begging him not to do it. Sweetie holds his sword up, ready to decapitate me.

"Go ahead!" I yell. "It won't work! Cut off my head! See if I care!"

Sweetie slices his sword and my head falls to the ground. Much as Sweetie predicted, my headless torso squirts blood up in the air for a moment before it collapses to the ground. The audience explodes in outrage.

"That didn't hurt!" I holler. "Loser!"

Frowning, Sweetie Honey picks my severed head up off the ground. He removes the scarf and hood. His shoulders fall.

"I'm fine, everybody!" I announce. "Don't worry about it! I'm good! Please, retake your seats and calm down!"

Sweetie drops the head and looks around the stadium, probably wondering where I'm hiding.

"That wasn't me," I explain. "It was an actor I paid to play the part of me. I'm sorry to deceive you like that, but I get really nervous in front of big crowds, especially when

N V P F Z

I'm supposed to appear before one on the same day a ninja detective has made an appointment to kill me. To help with my nerves, I'm taking anti-anxiety medication. I mix it with hard liquor, which they say is a bad idea, but it's not. It's actually a really good idea. Anyway, I'm sorry I couldn't be there with you today. I'm on my aircraft carrier, safe and sound, speaking to you live via satellite, watching what's happening in (quote unquote) real (quote unquote) time on a wall of monitors. I've got all kinds of different angles here. I can zoom in if I want. Then I can zoom out. Zoom! See that? Zoom! Can they see that? No? Okay, well. It's pretty awesome! Anyway, Sweetie Honey didn't kill me. He killed an innocent actor. It's a tragedy, obviously, but you know, whatever. Stuff happens."

In a puff of smoke, Sweetie Honey disappears from the stadium and my wall of monitors.

CHAPTER SEVENTEEN:
Farm-Raised People

After the speech at the stadium, I decide to act on some intelligence I received about a zombie-run farm that grows people. No. I'm determined to act on it. Ninja detective or no ninja detective, I *must* act on it. A helicopter takes us from my aircraft carrier to the mainland.

In a pickup truck in the night, driving down a dirt road, with headlights shooting sight in front of us and a bit off to the sides, where scant crops struggle against the elements and because of those elements, and amongst and in them, a couple of my hot young female followers and I smoke and drink and listen to pirated music too loud. The windows are rolled down. The outside rushes in, swirling everything around. I've got the Pope's hat trapped between my knees so it doesn't blow away. Beneath the truck, dust grows. Behind the truck, dust glows. We're in the country. In the heart of it. The side. The countryside. We're in the broken breadbasket zombies try to hold together while pulling it apart.

We skid to a stop at a farm in the nowhere of the middle. There are twelve pickup trucks in my convoy: all of them full of my girls. The dust we make catches up with us. We do up our windows. We cough. We blink. The trucks' headlights illuminate the particles before us.

When it clears, I see them—the babies: the fields full of ripe babies. Their heads stick out of the dusty brown earth in rows. The headlights illuminate them and give them long shadows. The shadows angle off in different directions because of how the trucks are parked. The babies wear the soil like clothes. The clothes come up to their chins. The babies disappear beneath the earth. All the infants' eyes are closed. They're not alive yet. They're not people. They haven't been picked.

"You know where babies come from?" I ask the followers in my truck. I keep staring straight ahead through the windshield.

They know where babies come from: there's hardcore zombie pornography playing on my ceremonial robe. "Where do babies come from?" they ask.

I put on the pirated Pope's pirate hat. I open the truck's door. "Bad luck," I answer, getting out.

Some of the baby heads have thin tufts of hair. Most are hairless. Some are dark skinned. Others light. Some have heads that look too small. Others too big.

When we're all gathered, I tell my followers, "Let's get to work."

We start picking the babies out of the dirt and throwing them into the backs of pickup trucks. The babies don't wake; they don't cry. They're vegetables: silent, unresisting. When I grab a head in the palm of my hand and pull the shoulders through the soil and shake off the clumps of dirt, I can't believe this is how everything started for me. I can't believe I was one of these. I can't believe I was once this small and now I'm this big. I can't believe there was a time when I didn't know anything. I can't believe the idiocy I learned. I can't believe the lies I believed. I can't believe I still believe in anything. And yet.

I do.

Zombies *love* babies. "She's beautiful." "He's so cute." I don't do that. I don't judge babies on their appearances. I judge babies on their merits. I want to know what any given baby can do. The answer is usually, and sadly, the same: nothing. Babies are good for nothing. Unless you need someone to sleep prodigiously, eat voraciously, have remarkable difficulty belching, but absolutely no problem screaming, crying, and soiling him or herself, babies are essentially useless. But only to the untrained eye. The trained eye sees (a nice light snack or) future zombies.

All these writhing masses of selfishness can be taught, trained, and turned into future zombies. They must learn restraint, patience, and selflessness. (Babies are communists! They think everything should be done *for* them! "I'm hungry! Get over here!" "My diaper is wet! Change me!") They must *learn* to be zombies (or unlearn to be human). The zombie doesn't *only* think of itself. The zombie *also* thinks of what (it's told) is good for all. When it does something resembling an expression of self-interest, like eating, it's really just keeping its strength up so it can keep being a zombie—so it can keep creating more zombies.

Every once in a while, a baby doesn't quite make it into the back of a pickup. It falls on the ground. It bounces, limbs flailing, and rolls up against a tire, or under a truck. Or it slams into the side of the truck's box and drops straight down to the ground. The sound of baby on metal makes a memorable sound. It's a cross between a clang and a thump. A small group of my followers has a brief baby fight. They throw babies at each other. They fling the things by their arms and legs. They hold them by their heads and spin around and launch them. One of them sees me working, not playing, and watching them. A baby bangs into her chest, knocking her back a step. The baby falls to the ground in front of her. She picks it up, throws it into the back of a truck, and gets back to work. Crouched down, sticking my first and middle fingers into their eyeballs, I pick up two babies at the same time, one from a row on either side of me, and pull their bodies, dropping dirt, from the ground. I launch one at the girl who resumed working. It hits her square in the side of the head and knocks her down. I hold up my arms in victory: my free arm and the one holding the limp body of the unborn. "I win!"

Nearby, my raven perches on a fencepost, turning its head back and forth, observing everything through one black eye, and then the other. Sometimes it tips its head to the side, listening.

There's something satisfying about all this. There's something (non-intellectually) rewarding about working before the sun does. There's something (irrationally) pleasing about working after the sun quits for the day. (The sun never rises or sets; it only looks like it does.) Is it the dirt under my fingernails? Is it the sweat on my brow? Is it (not me personally) making something? Taking a seed, planting it, helping it grow, watching it, waiting for it, and then picking the fruits of labour? Is it eating it? Tasting what was grown? Is it selling it? The (not really) free exchange of goods among (not really) equals? Is it knowing so many are dependent on these efforts? Those suit-wearing, expensive-car-driving, city types. Is it knowing something they don't? Is it being certain that no matter what big ideas they have, what remarkable thoughts, they couldn't consider anything other than these efforts if these efforts were to suddenly stop? Could they get in a crop to save their lives?

This land is your land? No. This land is *my* land.

A half hour into pirating someone's crop, I stop, take

off my pirated Pope's pirate hat, and wipe my forehead with the back of my forearm. In one hand, I hold the Pope's hat. In my other hand, I hold a baby. I hold it by its head. Eyes closed, silent, limp, it dangles. Knowing nothing. Not even wondering.

As we drive off in twelve pickup trucks, a few babies drop off there and here in the rear view mirrors—we piled them too high—and they shoot backwards, limbs flailing, on the dirt road and get run over by the truck following. The bodies are too small. The bones are too soft. When you run one over, you don't even feel it.

We take the newly plucked to a big pit we dug in another field earlier in the evening. We unload. Afterward, when the gasoline is poured, the match is struck, and the pit burns hot and orange and bright and high into the night sky, reflecting back down off the clouds, I turn to one of my followers and say, "Did you know that vegetables are made of exactly the same things as people?"

"No."

"Even soy beans. Same as people."

"Wow."

"We're all cannibals." I walk over to a truck. "You have to kill *something* to live," I call back. I pull open the door, climb in, and shut the door behind me. I stare at the inferno in front of me. What is. I stare at the hell before me. What was. I stare at what I hope will be.

My raven lands on the hood of the truck. It stands there for a moment, looking at me. I like where its feathers end and its legs begin; it looks like it's wearing pirate breeches. My raven walks to the edge of the hood. It craps white on the pickup truck in the night.

I close my eyes and try not to think about it. About us. The monsters, the future monsters, and the monster food:

N V P F Z

The (sometimes) living, breathing, walking (occasionally coherently) talking, gene machines that want little more than to avoid negative stimuli and find positive stimuli and then blindly reproduce so only a paltry half of their genes survive in an eternal dwindling, which will ultimately lead to only one truly successful set of genes, or to a group of mutations that are smart enough and strong enough to enslave everyone, gather the lion's share of positive stimuli, and keep it for themselves, even though they can't possibly use it all, and then simply store it, luxuriating in just a small portion of it, while all the others starve but blindly reproduce anyway. I try not to think about us eating ourselves alive until there's nothing left but waste. The waste of waste.

My raven caws in warning.

I hear the pickup truck's driver's side door open. When I open my eyes, I see Sweetie Honey climbing in with me. My shoulders fall. I should've known better than to trust intelligence! This was a trap!

The raven stands on the edge of the truck's hood, watching as my death nears. The raven is ready to take flight when my death arrives.

Sweetie is dressed in his dark red ninja outfit. His sword is unsheathed and he's holding it. I wonder if he's smiling under his ninja hood.

"Why'd you just steal a bunch of lettuce and burn it?" asks Sweetie, settling into the driver's seat, closing the door behind him.

"It wasn't lettuce," I sigh, turning and looking straight ahead through the windshield at the hell before me and, juxtaposed against it, the raven. "It was babies."

Sweetie looks at the side of my face for a long time. Then he says, "It doesn't matter. I'm going to kill you now."

"All right. Just make it quick."

He pauses. "Someplace you need to be?"

"No. I just don't want a slow, painful death."

"Oh. Okay."

I close my eyes, scrunch up my face, and wait for it, not knowing what I'm waiting for or if I'll recognize it when it arrives. Then, dramatically, all of a sudden, totally out of nowhere, and to my utter astonishment, absolutely nothing happens.

"Are you going to do it?" I ask, with my eyes still closed and my face still scrunched.

"I can't," says Sweetie Honey.

"Because you're a little bitch?" I open one eye and look over at him.

"No."

"Just checking." I relax.

"I can't kill you because I love you, Man." He's staring at me very intently. "When I thought I'd decapitated you in the stadium, I was filled with a tremendous sense of loss and remorse. Not because, instead of killing you, I killed a poor, innocent actor. I was filled with a tremendous sense of remorse and loss because I thought I killed *you*. I love you, Guy Boy Man. I love you in a very gay way." In his mask, I see his eyes. In his eyes, I see a plea.

I don't say anything right away. I just take it in. Not like that. No. I just think about what he's said. Everything makes sense now. Well, not everything. But the pictures of shirtless hunks in his locker make sense. And it makes sense he wasn't tempted by the four Eastern European girls.

"Jeez. I'm flattered, Honey. I'm sorry, though. I've chosen to be heterosexual."

Sweetie's shoulders fall. He turns away, staring out into the night. "I understand."

"Do you want to be my homoerotic sidekick?"

"I guess." Sweetie is unmistakeably dejected.

I put my hand on his shoulder and give him an encouraging little shake. "Come on, Honey. I could really use your help."

"I can't stand the idea of being away from you," sighs Sweetie. "So I will assist you. And every once in a while, I'll look at you longingly."

"Cool."

A few moments pass in uncomfortable silence.

Finally, Sweetie says, "Since we're no longer enemies, I feel obliged to tell you I never had sexual relations with Baby Doll15. The only physical contact she and I ever had was that phony kiss we shared in front of my locker in the hallway of Scare City High that day, in hopes of making you crazy with jealousy."

I feel like I'm spinning, like I'm on a spinning planet spinning around a star spinning around the centre of a galaxy, which I am, obviously, but I feel it, and I feel it all of a sudden. I put my hands up on the roof of the truck, trying to keep from falling up into the dark sky.

Is everything lost between Baby Doll15 and I, or have we merely been separated because of a ninja's (presumably recompensed) treachery? Are we still separated now merely due to a series of unfortunate miscommunications? Is there hope for us? Can we be together again? Can we be together again as we never were before? Forever?

No. I still can't tell her I love her. Or I'll lose all my money. Plus I ruined everything. I thought Sweetie Honey was having sex with Baby Doll15, so I had sex with Sweetie Honey's mom a bunch of times. Now it turns out Sweetie Honey wasn't having sex with Baby Doll15, but I still had sex with his mom a bunch of times. Then, to make matters worse, which doesn't seem possible, I showed Baby Doll15 a recording of all the sex I had with Sweetie Honey's mom.

"You should talk to her," advises Sweetie. "Not my mom. You should never talk to, see, or in any way have any contact with my mother. You should talk to Baby Doll15."

"I can't. My life is a mess. I want better for her."

"What about what she wants?"

"Just let it go, Sweetie." I stick my hands in my crazy hair and pull. Then I say, "Hey. Where's my hat?"

"What hat?" says Sweetie.

"Funny." I open one hand between Sweetie and me, and wave my fingers toward myself a few times like, let's have it.

"I really don't know what you're talking about." Sweetie crosses his arms. He turns away.

"Sweetie, are you the Pope's homoerotic sidekick or mine?"

Sweetie just sits there for a while.

Then, reluctantly, Sweetie sticks his hand down the front of his pants and pulls out my hat. He passes it over to me, without looking at me. I put it back on.

I notice the crowd of hot young girls standing around the truck, staring at Sweetie and me, terrified. "It's okay!" I call out to them through the window, waving at them through the windshield. "I'm not dead!"

One of them calls back, "We didn't know what to do! We saw Sweetie get in the truck! We were so scared! One of us remembered seeing animals at a nearby farm so we ran over there and sacrificed a goat for you!"

"Good thinking!" I holler.

"The farmer saw us so we had to run like hell!"

"Okay!" I call, waving again.

"It might've been a dog!" calls one of them.

I don't know what to say, so I just wave some more.

"What do you want to do?" asks Sweetie.

I flop my head back against the headrest and glance over at him. Then I lazily look out the windshield at my hot young female followers comforting each other. "Are you any good as a detective?" I ask.

"I'm a *ninja* detective," says Sweetie, and snorts.

"No, I know. And you're an excellent ninja. I've seen your work. But I don't know if you're any good as a detective."

Sweetie turns to me and explains, patiently, "Okay, see, when I said I was a 'ninja detective' just then I was using 'ninja' in that instance as an adjective to suggest that, as a detective, I'm incredibly good, even though I'm a ninja too."

"As a detective, you're ninja good?"

"Exactly," says Sweetie.

"So let me get this straight." I roll my head to the side. I stare at Sweetie. "Please, don't think I'm doubting you or anything. I just want to make sure we're on the same page: you're a real detective. You bag evidence, follow up on leads, bust perps, and that kind of thing?"

"Clues," says Sweetie, nodding. "I'm always on the lookout."

"All right." I roll my head away. "I've been having a hard time discerning the whereabouts of my arch enemy The Principal. To be honest, I haven't tried that hard, assuming the task would be herculean, since herculean tasks are the only kind I take on, because I'm a lot like Hercules. Anyway. The only thing I have to go on is that someone hired you to derail my plans. Who?"

"I don't know," says Sweetie, starting the truck. "But I know where we can find out."

CHAPTER EIGHTEEN:
The Ninja Agency

Sweetie stops the truck in front of an inauspicious-looking office building. He puts it in park. He turns off the engine. "TNA," he says, leaning forward and looking through the windshield at the building stretching up into the dark. "The Ninja Agency. Not TNA: The Ninja Academy."

I check out the building too. "She's not much of a looker."

"I don't know if you've noticed this about ninjas," says Sweetie, snidely, "but we don't like to stick out." He opens the door and puts a foot down on the ground, silently. "Things that stick out have a tendency to get cut off."

I frown, thinking about that. Then I open the door and get out.

Sweetie walks toward the building.

"It's the middle of the night," I say to Sweetie, catching up to him at the building's front. "It won't be open, will it?" I reach my hand out to try the door.

Sweetie grabs my wrist, stopping me. He holds it for a long time, looking at me in a way I consider curious.

He lets go of my wrist. He puts one finger over my lips.

Yes. It's weird.

I don't remember locks being picked. I don't remember

doors being opened. I don't remember going inside. All I know is, I'm inside now, with my back pressed flat against the wall. (I have a faint recollection of something I thought should click but that didn't.) I move my eyeballs in their sockets as quietly as I can. There's no one in here, as far as I can tell, which means, obviously, the place is crawling with ninjas! Of course! It's the middle of the night! When do ninjas do stuff? In the middle of the night!

The next thing I know, I'm facing the floor, about eight feet off the ground. I don't look over my shoulder (in case my neck cracks) but I know Sweetie Honey has his back almost pressed to the ceiling (not actually touching it because the fabric of his outfit might brush against it); he's doing the splits so his feet are flat on both sides of the hall's walls, near the top; his hands are flat on the walls too; and he's found some way to attach our bodies so we're both facing the same direction. I don't know if I'd rather be in this position, or face-to-face with him, in such close proximity. (I'm cool with it and everything; I just want it to be over soon.)

Our journey is neither fast nor slow. It stops and starts. We're near the ceiling in a hallway one moment, hanging there for no apparent reason, and then, the next moment, we're in a darkened custodial closet and Sweetie is peering through the crack he's opened the door. One second he's dragging me as he climbs an elevator cable; the next second we're in an air duct, waiting for some danger I can't see to pass.

We finally slip into a dark office on (what I guess is) the top floor. Sweetie replaces the ceiling tile.

Suddenly a male voice in the dark asks, "Why are you in my office?"

"That's a valid question and I'm going to be completely honest with you," I say. "I don't know why I'm in your office"—I start thinking about it—"if this is, in fact, your office! As you claim! Okay. I realize that sounds a little paranoid. I'm sorry. That wasn't very polite of me. I'm sure this is your office. I just. I have trust issues when it comes to dealing with ninjas."

"It isn't my office," admits the male voice. "It's my secretary's office. I have to pass through it on the way to my office and I sensed your presence before I even entered."

"Right on."

"I said it was my office to keep you off balance."

"Nice."

"So what can I do you for?"

"Can we turn on the lights or something?"

"No."

"Okay. Well, I'm here with Sweetie Honey. I don't know why he's being so quiet. That was stupid. He's being so quiet because he's a ninja. I just thought, since this is The Ninja Agency, he'd take the lead in any conversations, and I find myself a little unprepared for this high-level talk. The darkness is also kind of messing with me. Sweetie?"

"You double-booked the stadium," says Sweetie, annoyed.

"You weren't supposed to be at the stadium," says the male voice in the dark. "That was personal on your part. Besides, Sweetie. We double-book all the time. You know that."

"I don't like it," says Sweetie. "I had to kill a bunch of my colleagues in that stadium."

"I don't like it, either," I say, following Sweetie's lead. "I paid a lot of money for those crappy ninjas. They just got massacred. Anybody can get massacred. I wanted ninjas! Awesome ninjas! Is that where I went wrong? I didn't specify I wanted ninjas of a certain calibre?"

N V P F Z

Everything goes quiet. I don't think anything happens, but this could be a bustling ninja hub and I'd never know it, because they're so quiet and it's damn dark in here.

"Those were good people," says the unidentified male voice. (I'm sure it's been identified previously by someone other than myself, although maybe it hasn't been, so never mind.)

"I suppose it depends on your definition of 'good people,' " I say.

Sweetie says, "I need to know who put me on Guy Boy Man's case."

"I can't tell you that. Our records are confidential."

"Please?"

"Okay. Let me just check his file."

A few seconds pass during which I assume the unidentified male voice uses his hitherto unseen corporeal form to obtain, peruse, and absorb the necessary information.

"Here it is," says the male voice. "Guy Boy Man was targeted by someone known as 'The Principal.' "

"I knew it!" I clench my fist.

"I made air quotation marks when I said 'The Principal,' but you didn't see. I assume you want his whereabouts too? Checking, checking. Here we go. The Principal can be found in The Principal's Office."

"Seems kind of obvious in retrospect," I admit.

"Anything else?" asks the male voice. "No? We're good? Okay. You'll see yourselves out? Great. Thanks. Oh, wait a minute. Do you mind telling me why I shouldn't just kill Guy Boy Man since you failed to derail his plans to end human suffering?"

"Flee, Sweetie, flee!" I yell, bravely. I run straight into a wall. I roll around on the floor for a while, holding my nose and cursing. Then, realizing the danger in which I still find myself, I feel around on the floor until I find my hat; clutching it in one hand, I start crawling. Unfortunately, I have no idea in which direction I should crawl. I get the distinct impression Sweetie and the person to whom the male voice belongs are watching me as plainly as if I was doing all this under bright lights. I crawl, bump into a wall, change direction, crawl some more.

"We can't kill him," says Sweetie.

"I'm pretty sure we can," says the male voice in the dark. "You hold him."

"No," says Sweetie. "We can't kill him because I love him."

I almost stop crawling when Sweetie says that. Out of respect. But I keep crawling. Out of courage.

"What about The Principal?" asks the male voice. "He hasn't got his money's worth. I've got to think about TNA, Sweetie."

"Let me worry about The Principal," I say, crawling in heroic circles.

After a slight hesitation, the male voice says, "Make sure he does, Sweetie. Make sure he worries a lot."

CHAPTER NINETEEN:
I Don't Need An Appointment Because I'm A Ninja

We have to wait for the school to open, so we go back to my castle and play videogames for a while. Then we get in my bulldozer and go out for a nice breakfast. Finally, we head to the school. That's when I see a bunch of zombies ambling out of the gymnasium.

"What's going on?" I ask.

"The Zombie Acceptance Test was today," says Sweetie Honey, lifting his chin at them.

"I totally forgot," I say. "Look at all these new zombies." I watch them stagger away from the school in a group. Their tests have already been graded. They've passed, and they've already been infected with "the Strain." Now they're undead. Their eyes are glazed over: white. Their skin is cold-looking and grey. They don't have any wounds yet from fighting with people who escaped the test and their children, but they will soon enough. Their clothes are stained blood-red from the students who didn't pass the ZAT. You can almost still hear the screams in the air.

Then I really do hear screams. They're my own. It takes me a while to figure out why I'm screaming but then I do.

I see Baby Doll15 in the crowd of zombies. She's become one of them. She took the ZAT. She's staggering forward, mindlessly.

Sweetie Honey is holding me back. I'm trying to get out of the bulldozer. I'm trying to get to her. Where is her unicorn? Why didn't it protect her from this?

Baby Doll15 is a beautiful zombie. Her arms are stretched out in front of her, reaching for something she'll never find. Her pale skin is even paler than usual. Her light-coloured eyes are now completely white. Her pink hair is brighter than ever. It's as vivid as the blood smeared over her face and down the front of her white shirt.

I slump back in my seat, devastated. My mission isn't so straightforward anymore. Now I have to find a way to turn zombies back into living people. Then I'm going to tell Baby Doll15 I love her. No matter what it costs me.

Sweetie Honey and I sit in my bulldozer and watch the zombies and Baby Doll15 stumble away from Scare City High. They get the rest of the day off after taking the ZAT. Sweetie and I watch them amble away, moaning, with their arms outstretched, until we can't see them anymore.

Then we get out and go looking for The Principal.

We find his office at the end of a long hall in Scare City High. It's a hitherto undiscovered administrative area of the school. The hall gets less and less ruinous and more and more pristine the closer we get to The Office. It's obvious this is where the money is. It's blatant where control lies. The handrail in the hall changes from rotten wood to burnished gold. The floor switches from broken glass and fallen ceiling tiles to impeccably clean highly polished dark hardwood. The walls turn from obscenity covered and blood splattered to sparkling jewel-encrusted. That really gets me upset. I could live with the burnished gold handrails.

N V P F Z

I could tolerate the highly polished dark hardwood floors. But sparkling jewel-encrusted walls? It's too much! I'd already vowed to put an end to this waste, but now I renew my vows!

Next to me sidesteps my sidekick, Sweetie Honey, dressed as the ninja he is. I've washed my face since I ran into a wall. There was a bit of dried blood in my nose. I'm okay now. I appreciate your concern. I'm wearing the Pope's hat and my ceremonial robe. As we traverse the length of the hallway leading to The Principal's Office, I carry one of my handguns at the ready.

Soon I will be face to face with Him. And, God willing, I'll end his reign of terror. (The Principal's reign of terror, not God's.) I will change his regime. (The Principal's regime; forget I mentioned God.) I will take his throne. (I won't occupy it; I'll destroy it, unless it turns out this school is at a certain stage of its development that requires an iron fist, then I'll get someone else to occupy the throne and I'll tell him or her what to do and say.) This is America. We don't have royalty like they do in France and San Francisco. We don't value people on the merits of their birth. Unless they were born to rich people. Or they were born with natural gifts.

At the end of the hallway, before we cross the threshold, Sweetie and I exchange a look. Sweetie gives me a slightly different look than I give him. Then I try to kick down the doors! It doesn't work! So I pull open the magnificent engraved wood double doors and leave them open! It'd be polite to close them but I don't because I'm pretty bad-ass!

Sweetie walks up to a plump woman working behind a desk in the outer office. (She's probably plump living off monies that were supposed to be geared toward our education, which is okay with me, really, because I disapprove of that education, even if it were to be delivered in the kind of environment better funding could provide.)

"Can I help you?" asks the plump woman, politely, looking up at us.

I point my handgun at her. "We're here to see The Principal."

"Do you have an appointment?"

"No. Is that necessary?"

"I'm afraid so," she says, making an apologetic face.

"Damn," I say, still pointing my handgun at her. "When is he free?"

She leafs through an appointment book. "I can get you in late next week. Is that okay?"

"Morning or afternoon?" I ask.

"I don't need an appointment because I'm a ninja," interrupts Sweetie.

"Oh," says the secretary. "I'm sorry. Go right in."

Sweetie and I burst into The Principal's Office, after knocking politely!

Now I can see him for what he is! A short, slender man! I thought he'd be overweight! And taller! I also thought he'd be a zombie! It seems the zombies are using this small man with thinning hair and delicate-looking round glasses! Still, he's a formidable foe! Not in a traditional sense, obviously!

"Guy Boy Man," he says, cheerfully, hurrying from behind his desk to usher us inside. "Come in, my dear boy. You brought Sweetie Honey? Wonderful!"

"I'm here to stop you!" I declare, pointing my handgun at him, but still taking the seat he kindly offers me. "No longer will you be able to turn me and my fellow students into zombies or zombie food! No longer will we have to listen to your announcements! Your pronouncements! No longer will we have to endure your reminders about sporting events and academic competitions! Maybe we don't want to register, sign up, or try out! Did you ever think of that?"

"You make some salient points, my dear boy!" croons The Principal, hurrying back behind his desk and taking a seat. "Is there any way I can convince you to turn your charismatic leadership toward student politics? I think you'd make a wonderful Class President!"

"You think I'd be good? Really? That's nice of you to say. I appreciate your kind words, specifically about my grace under pressure, and my rhetorical skill. However, I'm afraid I have to spoil your party, Principal!" I point the gun at him in a slightly more menacing way.

The Principal doesn't say anything. Smiling, interested, he just looks at me and the handgun. Then he looks at Sweetie Honey who's sitting next to me on the arm of my chair. (I don't know why he's sitting on the arm of my chair. Why isn't he sitting in the empty chair next to mine? We're going to have to talk about that later.) Still smiling, The Principal looks back at me and the handgun I'm pointing at him.

"This is a lot less dramatic than I thought it would be!" I announce.

"How so?" asks The Principal, genuinely interested.

"Well, you know, I thought there'd be a big fight."

"Between the two of us?" laughs The Principal. "Oh, my dear boy." He leans back in his oversized genuine leather chair and touches the fingertips of both hands together. "I'm not the fighting kind. Besides, your quarrel isn't with me, it's with the school board."

"Why don't you just kill him and get it over with?" sighs Sweetie Honey.

"I can't just shoot him, can I?" I whine. "I mean, he has to put up a fight or something, doesn't he? We're arch enemies. I'm holding up my end of the arch or whatever you do with arches. He's totally failing on his side of the arch. It's, like, half an arch. What do you have when you halve an arch?"

"You could give him a head start," suggests Sweetie.

"And then hunt him down and kill him?" I frown. "How is that more humane?"

"It gives him a chance," says Sweetie, and shrugs.

"Yeah," I say. "A chance to escape. Thanks for your help, Sweetie. Jeez. I finally find the despicable tyrant responsible for all our suffering and you want me to let him go?"

"As I was trying to say," interrupts The Principal, looking at us over the rims of his small circular glasses, "your quarrel isn't with me; it's with the school board.

"All right." I point my gun at The Principal again. "Where is this school board?"

"I'll happily give you the home addresses of the school board members, my dear boy," says The Principal, opening a drawer in his desk. "But you should know before you go, the school board is answerable to higher-ups, and they have higher-ups, who, in turn, have higher-ups."

"Wait a minute," says Sweetie, narrowing his eyes at The Principal, suspiciously. "What are you saying?"

In an astonished hush, I whisper to Sweetie, "This could go all the way to the mayor!"

Instead of a list of names and addresses, suddenly The Principal pulls a missile launcher from the desk drawer! I say "suddenly" but it's actually taking quite a while because it's big and heavy. It's a pretty tight fit in the desk drawer. The Principal has to try angling it out in a couple of different directions before he gets it free. There's a lot of banging around while he's doing that. I should've mentioned earlier that this particular desk drawer is a lot bigger than a normal-sized desk drawer. "We confiscated this from a student last week," says The Principal.

Instead of shooting The Principal while he's wrestling with a cumbersome piece of military hardware and a strangely shaped piece of furniture, I just stare at Sweetie Honey, still astonished—less astonished that this could go all the way to the mayor, although that's pretty astonishing, and more astonished that 1) The Principal has a missile launcher; 2) he's getting it; 3) it seems to have a missile in it; 4) he's levelling the loaded missile launcher at Sweetie Honey and, more importantly—no offense, Sweetie—me; 5) The Principal is just as bad-ass as I thought he was going to be; 6) The Principal somehow tricked me into thinking he isn't that bad-ass; 7) I'm an idiot; 8) I think I should probably shoot The Principal before he pulls the trigger or whatever you do to launch a missile from a missile launcher; 9) why doesn't Sweetie kill The Principal?; 10) why do I always have to do everything?; 11) if Sweetie isn't going to kill The Principal, shouldn't he find a place to hide?; 12) shouldn't I find a place to hide?; 13) that's an awesome missile launcher; 14) I can't believe The Principal has an awesome loaded missile launcher and he's pointing it at me and I'm just standing here like an idiot next to a handsome homosexual African-American ninja detective named Sweetie Honey who loves me and who's just standing there like an idiot even though The Principal is pointing an awesome loaded missile launcher at him too: he's actually kind of pointing it in between Sweetie and me but that's probably because you don't need to be that specific with a missile launcher; you just point it in the general direction of everything you want to blow up and it looks after that for you.

"Class dismissed," says The Principal. Then he launches the missile.

The following happens rather quickly and in a space

which, although it contains a number of violent actions, seems strangely still. The missile shoots from the tube. It's accompanied by a whoosh too loud to be considered a whoosh. The projectile seems to have been spit like a student letting loose a wad of chewed-up paper. Mercifully, the missile passes between Sweetie and me. Indifferent, the rocket glares red and traces white out through the door I left open in a bad-ass way. Conveniently, the missile does a ninety-degree turn. It shoots through the other set of doors I refused to close because I'm so rebellious. I don't think I mentioned this earlier but there are windows in one of the jewel-encrusted walls leading to The Principal's Office, and through the corner of my eye, I see the missile streaking down the hall, heading for the school proper, beyond the administrative area where we are now. Right when it reaches the broken heart of Scare City High School, the missile explodes!

It explodes into all the classrooms! It explodes into all the desks and chairs and problems that were never solved at them, on them, and there! It explodes into the clocks and doors! It explodes into the ceilings that held us down and the floors that held us up! It explodes into everything that keeps us repeating the mistakes our parents made! It explodes into the past they left us and called the future!

The Principal is worming around, pinned beneath the missile launcher. Sweetie and I regain our feet, and I find my gun in the disturbed mess of the office.

"That was an inappropriately large explosion," says Sweetie, dusting himself off. "It's like someone was using the classrooms to store fireworks and barrels of gasoline."

"Obviously, we're going to have to do a lot of research to be certain," I say, "but I think we can safely designate today the most awesome day ever, including all the days involving Jesus." I hold up my hand for a high five.

"No," says Sweetie, rejecting my proffered high five.

I look at him, hurt.

"The most awesome day so far," he clarifies, "because we're about to embark on a series of adventures to get to the bottom of all this, and I suspect we have even more awesome days ahead." Then, illustrating the day's glory, as Scare City High burns, Sweetie high fives me more highly than a high five has ever before been given.

Then I walk through the ruins of the office to The Principal. Beneath the missile launcher, he lies squirming. His little round glasses are broken and askew on his little face. I stand over him, in judgement really, because I'm judging him, and I'm standing in a way which, if I considered it from his perspective—which I never would, because it'd be beneath me—would be beneath me. I point the gun at him again and say, in a really bad-ass way, "I'm shooting you out of principle."

I squeeze the trigger.

Nothing happens.

"Oh, come on," I say. I forgot to chamber a round, so I chamber a round, and I point the gun at The Principal again. He's still worming around; he's doing so in a very lowly way. (I'm trying to bring back any sense of supremacy I may have had and lost when we had the gun issue there a second ago.) So, yeah. I'm lording over him and everything—not that I think I'm God or anything. More a demigod, really. I'm probably a lot closer to God, level-wise, than I am to regular mortals. Anyway, from my position, physically and mentally, far, far above The Principal, I gaze down upon him, coolly, while pointing the gun at him, also coolly, but I'm thinking of a different kind of cool right here. "I'm shooting you out of principle," I say again. I go to squeeze the trigger, but then I realize there might be some confusion. "When I say I'm shooting 'you' out of principle, I'm not referring to some sort of spirit or soul I believe inhabits The Principal and that, when I shoot The Principal, will somehow be freed, perhaps to, happily, journey Heavenward, or get dragged, if a soul or spirit can be dragged, to Hell, although I believe all that crap. No. When I say I'm shooting you out of principle, I mean I'm shooting you because I really disagree with . . ."

"Just do it!" shouts The Principal, finally giving up his attempt to get out from under the missile launcher, which you should never do. You should never give up. Especially when you're stuck under something. You should just keep struggling and struggling until you die.

"Right," I say. "Okay. I'm going to shoot you now." I pull the trigger again. Nothing happens again. I curse for a while. Then I click off the safety.

"You're shooting me out of principle," says The Principal, waving his hand in a circular motion like, get on with it.

"Right," I say. I pull the trigger.

When it's done, Sweetie stands beside me. He puts his hand on my shoulder and says, "I know that was difficult for you, Man."

"Because of the gun?" I say. "Yeah. Stupid things. I mean, they're awesome, but . . ."

Sweetie Honey and I leave the ruined high school. Immediately, I start trying to figure out how to change Baby Doll15 back from a zombie to a living human being so I can tell her I love her, even though it means losing all my trillions. I know I'm going to hear it's impossible—it can't possibly work—but I'm going to do it anyway. I've got an idea about where to begin.

"Don't even think about it," says Sweetie.

The idea involves kicking Sweetie in the testicles.

Centaur111 told me that if I ever need to contact him, I should kick someone in the testicles. Centaur111 finds people getting kicked in the testicles hilarious and he always shows up, magically, just in time to see it.

There's a thirty-something zombie wearing jeans and a ripped T-shirt ambling around nearby. He's got a receding hairline and a pair of broken glasses. I hurry over to him and kick him in the groin as hard as I can. Right as I'm pulling my leg back, Centaur111 appears. His eyes and mouth are wide open, expectantly. The thirty-something zombie doubles over and falls to the ground, groaning, as soon as I kick him. He was groaning before I kicked him so that's not really a change. I don't know why I mention it.

Centaur111 howls with laughter.

"Hey, Centaur111, I need your help," I say.

"What's up?" he says, wiping a tear from his eye.

"I fell in love with a girl and I'm willing to give up my unimaginable wealth to tell her I love her, but she just became a zombie and I need to find a way to turn her back into a living human being. Can you help me?"

Centaur111 puts his hand on his chin and strokes it. "This was long-prophesied," he says.

"Really?" I say.

"No," says Centaur111. "I say 'long-prophesied' because it inspires more confidence. In truth, we only received the prophesy a short time ago. But, I contend, a prophecy is a prophecy no matter when it's received. In fact, 'recent' prophesies about 'near-future' events are surely more valuable than 'old' prophesies about events that 'might not happen' in our lifetime."

"That's true," I say.

"You're actually the one who made the prophesy, Guy Boy Man," says Centaur111. "In the future, you will travel back to the past, to Fairyland, to predict the future, which will really be more like telling what's happened to you lately."

Sometimes I forget I'm a prophet. Following a bunch of unnervingly accurate predictions, mostly about the outcome of cock fights, I had to relinquish my amateur "phet" status and was forced to turn pro.

"Tell me how to change Baby Doll15 back into a living girl," I say.

"You're asking if there's a cure for 'the Strain'?" says Centaur111. "You want to know if there's some way to reverse the effects of the virus that infects most people and turns them into zombies?"

"Yes," I say.

"No," he says. "There isn't. But don't let that discourage you. You, in your role as the Self-Appointed One, are destined to change all that. You're fated to find the cure. You told us this when you came back from the future." Centaur111 comes closer to me. "You remember when I gave you access to your fortune and I made you promise never to tell a girl you love her or else you'd lose all your wealth?"

"Yeah," I say. "That's what started all this trouble. If I could have just told Baby I love her, Sweetie never could have caused so much damage with that note."

"Well, it was actually your idea to tie the money to the promise to never tell a girl you love her."

"I made myself promise that?" I say, frowning.

"Yes," says Centaur111.

"Why?"

"You wanted to be really sure you loved her before you told her so."

"So I won't really lose my money when I tell Baby Doll15 I love her?" I ask.

"No," says Centaur111.

"Baby Doll15 became a zombie for nothing!" I say. I'm so angry with myself, for putting my money ahead of her. For sleeping with Sweetie's mom to get back at Sweetie and her. Will Baby Doll15 ever forgive me? "Did I tell you, in the future, how I'm going to find the cure for the Strain?"

"No," says Centaur111.

"God," I say. "I seem to have told you everything but."

"As you know from the series of exciting adventures you can't be bothered to relate here, there's a revolutionary faction of supernatural creatures in Fairyland intent on overthrowing the tyranny of the zombies and the shadowy figures that control them. We have a number of ideas about how to take the zombies down, but the idea we're most optimistic about is finding a zombie that hates being a zombie and manipulating him or her to learn who wields the real power in the zombie world. Obviously, once we find a zombie that hates being a zombie, he or she will be an excellent candidate for testing different ways of undoing the zombie virus. But we can't do any of this without your help, Guy Boy Man."

"You're talking about, like, financial help?" I ask, skeptically.

"We need you, Guy Boy Man," says Centaur111.

"You need, like, a few thousand dollars maybe?" I suggest, hopefully.

"Will you join us?"

"I'll do whatever it takes to get Baby Doll15 back," I say. And I mean it. I love her. I'd do anything.

"Then you and your ninja friend should accompany me to Fairyland where we'll begin laying the trap for a zombie that hates being a zombie."

TO BE CONTINUED IN

ZOMBIE VERSUS FAIRY
FEATURING ALBINOS

ACKNOWLEDGEMENTS

The author wishes to thank his agent, Liza Dawson, of Liza Dawson Associates Literary Agency, New York, for her insight, guidance, and support; Hannah Bowman for being right, Judith Engracia and Victoria Horn for always getting it done, and everyone at Liza Dawson Associates Literary Agency; Fernanda Viveiros for recommending ChiZine Publications; Erik Mohr for the amazing cover image; Laura Marshall for her great marketing ideas and help; Samantha Beiko for proofreading, doing the layout, and more; everyone at ChiZine Publications, especially co-publishers Brett Savory and Sandra Kasturi for pouring their hard work, time, and resources into *Ninja Versus Pirate Featuring Zombies*, thereby helping the author realize a dream: seeing it published. The author also wishes to express his gratitude to his friends and family.

The BC Arts Council and the Canada Council for the Arts provided assistance in bringing this project to fruition. Their help is deeply appreciated.

ABOUT THE AUTHOR

James Marshall's short fiction has appeared in numerous Canadian literary magazines: *PRISM International*, *The Malahat Review*, *Exile*, *The Literary Quarterly*, and *Prairie Fire*. One of his stories was nominated for the National Magazine Award for fiction, the M&S Journey Prize, and it was a finalist in the 22nd Annual Western Magazine Awards, 2004. A collection of his short stories, *Let's Not Let a Little Thing Like the End of the World Come Between Us*, was published by Thistledown Press in 2004, and it was shortlisted for both the 2005 Commonwealth Writers' Prize (Caribbean and Canada Region) in the 'Best First Book' category, and the ReLit Award for short fiction. James lives and writes in BC.

SHOEBOX TRAIN WRECK

JOHN MANTOOTH

AVAILABLE MARCH 2012
FROM CHIZINE PUBLICATIONS

978-1-926851-54-9

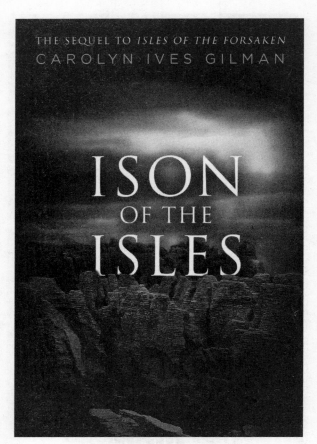

ISON OF THE ISLES

CAROLYN IVES GILMAN

AVAILABLE APRIL 2012
FROM CHIZINE PUBLICATIONS

978-1-926851-56-3

WESTLAKE SOUL
RIO YOUERS

AVAILABLE APRIL 2012
FROM CHIZINE PUBLICATIONS

978-1-926851-55-6

A TREE OF BONES

VOLUME THREE OF THE HEXSLINGER SERIES

GEMMA FILES

AVAILABLE MAY 2012
FROM CHIZINE PUBLICATIONS

978-1-926851-57-0

RASPUTIN'S BASTARDS
DAVID NICKLE

AVAILABLE JUNE 2012
FROM CHIZINE PUBLICATIONS

978-1-926851-59-4

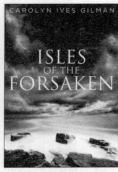

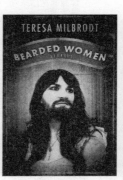
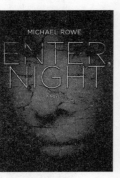

978-1-926851-10-5
TOM PICCIRILLI

EVERY SHALLOW CUT

978-1-926851-09-9
DERRYL MURPHY

NAPIER'S BONES

978-1-926851-11-2
DAVID NICKLE

EUTOPIA

978-1-926851-12-9
CLAUDE LALUMIÈRE

**THE DOOR TO
LOST PAGES**

978-1-926851-13-6
BRENT HAYWARD

**THE FECUND'S
MELANCHOLY
DAUGHTER**

978-1-926851-14-3
GEMMA FILES

A ROPE OF THORNS

CHIZINEPUB.COM CZP

978-0-9812978-9-7

TIM LEBBON

**THE THIEF OF
BROKEN TOYS**

978-0-9812978-8-0

PHILIP NUTMAN

CITIES OF NIGHT

978-0-9812978-7-3

SIMON LOGAN

**KATJA FROM THE
PUNK BAND**

978-0-9812978-6-6

GEMMA FILES

**A BOOK OF
TONGUES**

978-0-9812978-5-9

DOUGLAS SMITH

CHIMERASCOPE

978-0-9812978-4-2

NICHOLAS KAUFMANN

**CHASING THE
DRAGON**

"IF YOUR TASTE IN FICTION RUNS TO THE DISTURBING, DARK, AND AT LEAST PARTIALLY WEIRD, CHANCES ARE YOU'VE HEARD OF CHIZINE PUBLICATIONS— CZP—A YOUNG IMPRINT THAT IS NONETHELESS PRODUCING STARTLINGLY BEAUTIFUL BOOKS OF STARKLY, DARKLY LITERARY QUALITY."

—DAVID MIDDLETON, *JANUARY MAGAZINE*

978-0-9809410-9-8
ROBERT J. WIERSEMA

**THE WORLD MORE
FULL OF WEEPING**

978-0-9812978-2-8
CLAUDE LALUMIÈRE

**OBJECTS OF
WORSHIP**

978-0-9809410-7-4
DANIEL A. RABUZZI

THE CHOIR BOATS

978-0-9809410-5-0
LAVIE TIDHAR AND NIR YANIV

**THE TEL AVIV
DOSSIER**

978-0-9809410-3-6
ROBERT BOYCZUK

**HORROR STORY
AND OTHER
HORROR STORIES**

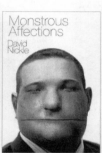

978-0-9812978-3-5
DAVID NICKLE

**MONSTROUS
AFFECTIONS**

978-0-9809410-1-2
BRENT HAYWARD

FILARIA

"CHIZINE PUBLICATIONS REPRESENTS SOMETHING WHICH IS COMMON IN
THE MUSIC INDUSTRY BUT SADLY RARER WITHIN THE PUBLISHING INDUSTRY:
THAT A CLEVER INDEPENDENT CAN RUN RINGS ROUND THE MAJORS IN
TERMS OF STYLE AND CONTENT."

—MARTIN LEWIS, *SF SITE*

ALSO AVAILABLE FROM CHIZINE PUBLICATIONS